D0262248

The Witch Doctor
Of Umm Suqeim

The Witch Doctor
Of Umm Suqeim

Craig Hawes

PARTHIAN

Parthian
The Old Surgery
Napier Street
Cardigan
SA43 1ED

www.parthianbooks.com

First published in 2013
© Craig Hawes 2013
All Rights Reserved

ISBN 9781908946706

Editor: Susie Wild
Cover by www.jesseboyce.co.uk
Typeset by Elaine Sharples
Printed and bound by Gomer Press, Llandysul, Wales

Published with the financial support of the Welsh Books
Council

British Library Cataloguing in Publication Data

A cataloguing record for this book is available from the
British Library.

For my parents

Contents

The Witch Doctor of Umm Suqeim

Jaydeep and Melody stood outside the villa looking in through the liquorice-twist rungs of the wrought iron gate on which hung some sort of Native American dreamcatcher device – a fan of pink flamingo feathers wound, with thread, to the shaft of a large barbed fishing hook.

'I suppose this is it, then,' Jaydeep said. Melody pulled a rumpled Post-it note from her handbag and again read it aloud. 'Last villa on 16b street. Palm tree outside. White garage door.' She nodded at the feathers. 'I think that's a bit of a giveaway, don't you?'

'He'll have us drinking menstrual blood from a monkey's skull,' Jaydeep said, studying the beige two-story building for any signs of life. He felt that if he listened closely enough he would hear from within its walls animals being sacrificed to the sound of incantations and frenziedly beaten drums.

Jaydeep had phoned the witch doctor two days before to make the appointment. Melody had been given his number by Noura, her Egyptian capoeira instructor and, given the amount of psychic mumbo-jumbo she was filling her head with, spiritual guru. The witch doctor, whose specialty was 'relationship healing', had brought a happy ending to a conjugal crisis where a year of hypnotherapy sessions and marriage guidance counselling had proved hopelessly ineffective. Noura hadn't stopped gushing about him since.

'Is this the, uh, witch doctor?' Jaydeep had enquired with the quiver-voiced uncertainty of a hunchbacked psoriasis sufferer asking Naomi Campbell on a date.

'If you think you have a problem that cannot be solved by the mortal abilities of therapists and doctors, then I can almost certainly help,' the man had said, after a cautious pause and in what sounded like a West African accent. 'But I'd prefer mystical warrior to witch doctor, an appellation that sounds quaintly primitive. And please... call me Mr N'Dengu.'

Mr N'Dengu had asked Jaydeep a few questions before confirming the early evening appointment. Among other things he'd wanted to know the nature of their problem, Jaydeep's ethnicity and, rather bafflingly, whether he was from a family dominated by men or women. He'd also wanted to know what Jaydeep did for a living and seemed a little unimpressed that he was a chef.

Still, Mr N'Dengu had seemed satisfied enough with the answers to accept them as clients. And now here they were in this well-kept Umm Suqeim street, the top half of the Burj Al Arab poking up above the rooftops of the villas.

A small red kite, fluttering in the wind, stood out against the rose-tinged sky. Jaydeep wondered who was flying it. Perhaps a father and his infant son, bonding on the beach. He craved that. From a young age he'd felt born to breed, that fatherhood would be the one thing in life he would revel in. As for Melody, she didn't so much want a child as need one to preserve her sanity. Recently she had taken to going inside baby shops whenever she passed one, making a mental note of the prices of prams and high chairs.

Yesterday after coming home from the restaurant where he worked Jaydeep had found her weeping in their spare bedroom. Currently a haven for Jaydeep's prized cricket memorabilia, it was long ago designated the future progeny's nursery, a haven of Disney wall-stickers and cuddly toys, its walls yet to be painted a gender-neutral lemon-yellow. 'I'll try anything,' Melody sobbed. 'IVF, shamans, witch doctors… I just want to be a mum, Jay.' And he had promised her that it would be okay, that they would explore every avenue, however unorthodox.

It struck him as odd that they were about to be helped in this quest by a practitioner of the occult, and yet the fertility clinic in London they had attended months previously, with its sterility and cold-palmed handshakes from the staff, was far more daunting – notwithstanding the slightly creepy voodoo-style paraphernalia hanging on the gate they now stood in front of.

Still, he wondered whether he would feel the same way if the witch doctor – or 'mystical warrior', as Mr N'Dengu preferred it – lived elsewhere. Whenever they read in the local newspapers about these people, they seemed to

3

operate out of the less salubrious parts of the city: Shindaga, Hor Al Anz or Ghusais. The upmarket address of Mr N'Dengu's villa and his rich vocabulary suggested he was of a different ilk to these gobbledygook-spouting charlatans and their comically elaborate scams.

They pressed the buzzer at the gate and gave each other thin-lipped smiles of reassurance.

'Look at us,' Jaydeep said, putting his arm around Melody's shoulders. 'Like Hansel and Gretel.'

A thin black woman on the cusp of old age led them into the villa and ushered them into a large dark room whose only window was covered with a purple sheet. She then left them alone without uttering a word. Whispering could be heard in another room before it was silenced by the gentle closing of a door.

A dozen or so small candles emitted enough light for them to make out pieces of hand-crafted wooden furniture, coffee-bean brown and draped with the skins of various exotic beasts, one of which, a leopard, still had its teeth-baring head attached. The candle flames reflected in its glass eyes seemed to give them life. It gave Jaydeep the creeps and he slyly trod on one of its paws to put his mind at rest.

In one corner of the room an elephant's foot had been fashioned into a table on which lay a chess set, its pieces made of ivory – or perhaps burnished bone. The room reeked of patchouli oil and candle wax, but also detectable was the sickly sweet scent of decay, which presumably came from the animal skins.

Jaydeep went over to the chessboard and picked up a pawn.

'Leave it alone,' Melody hissed.

'I wonder if he plays,' Jaydeep said, putting the pawn back on the wrong square.

'Keeps the mind sharp, I believe,' came a booming voice behind them.

Startled, Jaydeep and Melody turned around to find a man standing in the doorway. He was basketball-player tall and wore a black suit on top of a red silk shirt whose wide-open collar flopped over the lapels of the jacket. A silver chain sparkled amongst a salt'n'pepper furze of chest hair.

He strode into the room and the candle flames trembled in reverence. 'Joseph Makanga N'Dengu, at your service,' he said exuding confidence and shaking their hands before returning the pawn to its correct place on the chessboard. Jaydeep thought that he looked like something out of a seventies blaxploitation movie. Goatee beard, a short, neat afro and a cartoonishly large smile. The theme tune from *Shaft* started playing in Jaydeep's head, fading away only when Mr N'Dengu held on to Melody's hand longer than was entirely appropriate.

Mr N'Dengu told them to sit on the sofa and relax. He apologised for the dimness of the room but said the spirits he needed to call upon for his work had an aversion to bright light. He lowered himself into a wide leather chair opposite Jaydeep and Melody, stroking his beard as he studied each of them in turn. His eyes lingered on Melody a little longer than they did on Jaydeep, something that did not escape Jaydeep's attention. But then he was used to it, what with

Melody's seraphic beauty and Russian tennis player physique.

They sat in silence for several minutes before Mr N'Dengu spoke again.

'Hmmm, I sense great sadness in you both,' he said, sinking back in the chair and crossing his long legs. 'Your desire for a child is immense, it is plain to see, yet do not fear, I can assure you that in time you will become the proud... ah, but wait.' His eyes widened and his voice turned to a barely audible whisper. 'It lurks... amongst us.'

Mr N'Dengu shuffled forward to the edge of his chair. He removed a crucifix from around his neck and began massaging it with his fingertips. Closing his eyes, he jerked his head back as if some unseen force had given the nape of his neck a vicious yank.

'Oh, saviour take my side,' he said, his body shaking. 'Give me the strength to overcome this unholy fiend before me, this vile acolyte of Lucifer. Sssshhhhhnnnng-y-yes, yes, aaah! Imbue my mortal bones with your divine power! Yes-yes-aaah-yes, such power!'

At last the shaking subsided and he sat still, breathing rapidly through his nose. When Mr N'Dengu opened his eyes again they had the petrified look of a man who had just witnessed a medieval torture session. He seemed to be staring at a point somewhere above Jaydeep's head.

Jaydeep turned around to see what he was looking at, but there was nothing there except a photo on the wall of a young Mr N'Dengu in his college cap and gown. Jaydeep wondered from which dubious academic institutions you could obtain a qualification in the art of black magic. No doubt the same sort of place where you could get a degree in Media Studies.

'Jaydeep,' Mr N'Dengu said, his breathing normal again. 'You have acquired, I believe, an embittered and vengeful enemy, one who has sent a malevolent spirit to cause you immense harm.'

'No shit,' Jaydeep said.

'A fellow chef whose recipe you have stolen, perhaps?'

'Not in my nature, Mr N'Dengu.'

'A relative you have double-crossed, then?'

Jaydeep thought for a moment. 'I owe my uncle Ram two hundred quid but he knows I'm good for it.'

'Think, take your time, this is extremely important,' Mr N'Dengu said.

There was silence for a whole minute.

'What about Oliver?' Melody said at last.

'Who is Oliver?' Mr N'Dengu asked.

'Oh for fuck's sake, Mel!'

'Truth is essential, Jaydeep. Lies will render my powers impotent and you'll be wasting our time.'

Jaydeep looked at Melody who gave him a prompting nod.

'I was unfaithful, Mr N'Dengu,' Jaydeep said at last. 'Seduced by an older woman.'

'I forgave him,' Melody said.

'Continue, please,' Mr N'Dengu said.

Jaydeep looked down at the floor.

'He had sex with Nicole, Ollie's wife,' Melody said. 'Last year at the staff party.'

Jaydeep looked at Mr N'Dengu who stroked his beard and said: 'Hmhmm.'

'So now you know,' Jaydeep said. 'And yeah, he probably hates my guts. But we've all moved on, yeah? Water under the bridge. Anyway, they moved to Kuala Lumpur last month so—'

'Distance has no relevance,' Mr N'Dengu said.

'Hang on, you're saying Oliver's put some sort of... *curse* on me?'

'Almost certainly. A demon spirit lies beside you when you make love to your wife, preventing you from conceiving. This is undoubtedly Oliver's doing.'

The idea of a supernatural *ménage à trois* gave Jaydeep goosebumps. He visibly shivered.

'This city has several men like me,' Mr N'Dengu said. 'Sadly one or two are willing to abuse their powers for the right price. A disgrace to the profession. Oliver must have paid one of them handsomely.'

'Look, can you send this thing away or not, Mr N'Dengu?' Melody asked.

Mr N'Dengu scratched his head. 'It is possible, yes, but expelling demon spirits of this kind is a complex procedure.'

'How much are we talking, Mr N'Dengu?' Jaydeep said. 'To lift this curse, make this spirit go away?'

Mr N'Dengu laughed and put one hand on Jaydeep's shoulder. 'My brother, why do you insult me? My work is strictly non-profit. I neither want nor need your money.'

'Really?' Melody said.

'Of course! But there are materials I will need to put this spell in motion. Some strands of your hair, Melody – plucked not cut – and a photograph of the inciter of this heinous spell… Oliver, did you say his name was? A print-out of his Facebook profile photo will suffice. Lastly, and I do apologise if you find this distasteful, I'll need a semen sample from you, Jaydeep.'

'I'll give him a hand,' Melody joked, then blushed when Mr N'Dengu's face remained impassive.

'Let us reconvene a week today,' Mr N'Dengu said. 'Then we can proceed in earnest.'

Jaydeep and Melody looked at each other and nodded, and then the old woman came into the room as if she had been listening outside the whole time.

'Zeema, arrange their next appointment,' Mr N'Dengu ordered her. 'I must rest now and replenish my psychic energy before my next client, a Saudi businessman who wants me to cure his homosexual son. Such intolerance saddens me deeply, but if I can spare this poor young man from a public decapitation, well…' He shrugged his shoulders as he strode out of the room.

Zeema gave an apologetic smile, as if to atone for her employer's abrupt departure. 'I'll just need the consultation fee for today,' she said. 'Which is one thousand dirhams.'

Jaydeep took out his wallet and handed over the money.

'As Mr N'Dengu has informed you, his services are free,' Zeema said. 'However he will require some extra materials which need to be smuggled in from Africa.'

'Like what?' Melody said.

'Two grams of powdered rhinoceros horn, the heart of a female baboon, several rare herbs and a vial of water from a remote salt lake in Djibouti – none of which is available at your local pharmacy, obviously, which is why we rely on our Somalian contacts to bring it in on a dhow.'

'And all this amounts to what exactly?' Jaydeep said, checking the contents of his wallet.

Zeema produced a calculator from an inside pocket of her jacket and prodded the buttons with her withered fingers. 'Eight thousand, nine hundred and seventy two dirhams. And 75 fils.'

There was a sharp intake of breath from Jaydeep.

Zeema again went into her pocket and pulled out a tiny onyx camel. She placed it in Jaydeep's palm. 'We'll throw in this protective talisman free of charge. Believe me, you're going to need all the help you can get.'

*

Jaydeep, dick in hand, was trying to get aroused over a photograph of a skinny Japanese girl with black lipstick and a silvery-purple wig. He'd flicked through the magazine several times but few of the women in it did anything for him. At least this girl fondly reminded him of his university-era girlfriend, Yoshiko, the 'Nippon nympho' with a penchant for alfresco blowjobs. He'd even been faithful to her for a whole year. Apart from the one time with her flatmate.

He could hear Melody laughing downstairs at something Mr N'Dengu had said. Jaydeep resented the fact that Melody's contribution to N'Dengu's curse-lifting spell was a few wisps of her hair, while he had to degrade himself by tossing himself off to kinky Japanese porn (did that country even produce any other kind?), knowing that everyone in the villa – Melody, N'Dengu, Zeema – was aware he was doing so. Sure, it was probably nothing compared to the pain Melody would experience in childbirth. But women had been doing it for millions of years. If it was *that* traumatic why did so many end up having more than one? And these days you were given drugs to ease the pain. Free drugs. Time off work. Fathers didn't get such privileges.

They were back at Mr N'Dengu's villa exactly one week after their first appointment, armed with the items he had requested. Mr N'Dengu however had been concerned with the freshness of Jaydeep's semen. After its expulsion approximately 24 hours ago it had been carefully transferred to a plastic Nutella jar and put in the freezer. Unfortunately, due to a major traffic jam on Al Wasl Road and the car's air-con playing up, it had now spent well over an hour congealing in the 38-degree heat.

Mr N'Dengu said that this was such a frequent occurrence that he had turned his second bathroom into a makeshift 'masturbatorium', a room where male clients could produce a fresh supply, aided by some visual encouragement. This, Jaydeep discovered, consisted of three porn magazines and a badly illustrated copy of *the Kama Sutra*, a book that Melody had once posited, in all seriousness, as a way in which Jaydeep could reconnect with his Indian heritage.

After much deliberation Jaydeep had settled on the image of the Japanese girl, and half an hour after being sent to the masturbatorium, he had something to show for his efforts. He coyly handed it to a latex-gloved

Zeema who whisked it away 'for preparation'. Then he joined Melody and Mr N'Dengu in the darkened room where they were sitting next to each other on the sofa.

The second he entered they stopped talking.

'Ah, Jaydeep!' Mr N'Dengu said, standing up, 'welcome back.'

Jaydeep looked around the room. A large clay bowl filled with smouldering charcoal was placed atop the elephant's foot table. Next to it, on a small wooden trestle, were tiny cork-sealed bottles filled with indeterminate powders of various colours.

Mr N'Dengu was wearing the same suit as before but this time he wore a loose and colourful silk robe over it. This, he explained, was his ceremonial gown and had been handed down to him by his father, the great Akwanfe N'Dengu, a legendary magic man who had once prevented a constitutional crisis in a major West African country by changing the sex, *in utero*, of a tribal leader's baby. Melody tried to get him to elaborate on this but Mr N'Dengu was keen to press on with the ritual.

'Your presence is not required for this part,' Mr N'Dengu said. 'You may go home or wait outside, but your close proximity to the execution of the spell is strongly discouraged.'

'Come on,' Melody said to Jaydeep. 'Let's not jeopardise it.'

Shortly after they got home that evening they received a phone call from Mr N'Dengu. It was good news. The demon spirit, stubborn as it was, had shown definite signs of weakening.

Jaydeep, in celebratory mood, lit candles, opened a bottle of wine and put on a Ministry of Sound chill out CD.

'Not tonight, hun,' Melody said when Jaydeep had made some vaguely amorous advances. 'Let's wait until Joseph – I mean, Mr N'Dengu – says it's all over.'

Jaydeep reluctantly agreed. He hadn't had a decent night's sleep since the revelation that they were sharing their bed with one of Satan's poltergeist disciples, or whatever it was.

After five consecutive Friday afternoons of almost identical sessions, Mr N'Dengu said that the curse had been lifted for good and the demon spirit had fled their home. This was a huge relief to Jaydeep. He was getting fed up with visiting the masturbatorium every week, leaving Melody and Mr N'Dengu alone.

On their last ever visit he had found himself mysteriously locked in there after the door handle had got stuck. It took an hour for Zeema to find a screwdriver to dismantle it with her arthritic hands. In that time, Jaydeep later found out, Melody and Mr N'Dengu had gone to Starbucks for coffee.

'This and that' was Melody's vague reply when Jaydeep asked what they had talked about. Pressed to elaborate, she said that they had discussed a charity Mr N'Dengu was involved with in Africa which helped children injured by landmines.

'Ha! You don't believe that crap, do you,' Jaydeep said.

'Too right I believe it,' Melody said. 'You should see him when he talks about these poor kids, Jay. It's obvious that he's desperate to help them.'

'So our voodoo man is actually a Robin Hood character, fleecing Dubai's rich to help the destitute?'

'Would that be such a bad thing, when some dickheads here spend thousands on gold-plated iPads and cars decorated with Swarovski crystals. I mean, it's obscene.'

Jaydeep considered this for a moment and found himself unable to disagree.

'Well as long as he isn't fleecing *us*,' he said. 'I'm still not convinced he's got mystical powers.'

'I'm getting positive vibes from this guy,' Melody said. 'And Noura says he's got a violet aura, which is a sign of psychic power and attunement with oneself.'

'So the Sphinx is still riddling?' Jaydeep said, rolling his eyes.

They settled back into their daily routine, Melody at the drama college, Jaydeep at the Asian fusion restaurant in a four-star hotel where he worked as a commis chef. Jaydeep's late shifts meant that they barely saw each other at night. Melody was always asleep whenever he returned, bleary eyed and reeking of cooking oil. On the rare occasion they had sex, it was a 30-second, roll-on-roll-off job devoid of vigour. To Jaydeep's frustration, Melody's libido seemed to be wilting like an unwatered flower. This she blamed on the St John's Wort capsules and copious amounts of valerian tea she had started taking for her self-diagnosed mild depression.

'How are we going to get pregnant if you carry on like this?' Jaydeep asked one morning as she was getting ready for work.

'Me, not we.'

'It would be ours.'

'Just be patient,' Melody said.

'You're no spring chicken, Melody,' Jaydeep said. 'Tick-tock.'

Melody slapped him across the face and Jaydeep stared at her open-mouthed, clutching his cheek. He had never had her down as the slapping kind. Neither was he, but he found himself stepping towards her to retaliate, then thought better of it. He didn't put it past her to get Mr N'Dengu to put a spell on him. Premature baldness, perhaps. He had always been proud of his thick mane and Melody lamented the fact that his hair products took up more bathroom space than her own.

'If I'm going to have a baby it's going to have a happy mother,' Melody said, stomping out of the apartment and slamming the front door behind her.

Six weeks passed. Then, on a humid September evening while they were strolling around the boating lake in Safa Park, Melody announced to Jaydeep that she was pregnant. Jaydeep walked around in a bubble of elation for days, desperate to tell the whole world the joyous news. Preparing himself for the paternal challenge ahead, he set about ordering a load of child-rearing books off the internet and did research on the city's best antenatal clinics. Finally he put up for sale on eBay his entire cricket memorabilia which was all soon snapped up by a local Indian property tycoon. He gave the money to Melody, urging her to go on a spending spree to buy the baby things she had been eyeing for months. She pocketed the cash but said she'd wait until the annual shopping festival in the summer when everything could be had for bargain prices. Thinking that maybe she didn't want to tempt fate so early in the pregnancy, Jaydeep didn't force the issue. Besides, she'd been a little aloof with him recently. It was as if he'd been ousted by the unborn foetus as the most important person in her life. He was determined to get her back on side by indulging each of her new quirks, from the weird food cravings – cheese and onion crisps doused in Jif lemon juice – to the blog she had started writing about ethnic jewellery. Although he baulked at encouraging her sudden fascination with African literature.

'Name me one great African writer,' he asked her one evening.

'Wole Soyinka,' Melody said. 'Nobel Prize winner.'

'Never heard of him.'

'Can you name *any* living author who doesn't write about elves and warlocks?'

Jaydeep thought for a second. 'Is Salman Rushdie dead yet?'

*

One month later, Jaydeep was in a taxi, a stream of potential baby names running through the ticker tape of his mind (he'd always liked the name Mishal for a boy, Ambily for a girl), when a sporty little silver Audi pulled up next to him at the traffic lights on Baniyas Road. He was on his way to the spice soukh in Deira to pick up a kilo of turmeric powder, the weekly consignment from the hotel's regular supplier having failed to show.

The driver of the Audi was humming along to an old seventies funk number that Jaydeep loved. He asked the taxi driver to move forward so that he could get a better look at this man of impeccable musical taste. He was wearing large designer sunglasses and smoking a Cuban cigar, but there was no mistaking those chiselled features. Mr N'Dengu, Jaydeep had to admit, was an enviably handsome bastard.

It occurred to Jaydeep that Mr N'Dengu might be on his way to meet his Somali suppliers alongside the creek, where the old wooden dhows berthed. There would be a crate of African contraband in one of them. The withered innards of endangered animals. Rare plants from the barely penetrable jungles of central Africa. Vials of black mamba venom and curse-repelling crocodile tooth amulets.

The thought of witnessing the illicit transaction between Mr N'Dengu and these seafaring smugglers was too much for Jaydeep's curiosity to dismiss – which was why he ordered the taxi driver to follow him.

Mr N'Dengu parked his car in a small street in Naif, then began to walk towards the Creek. Jaydeep got out of the taxi a few yards away, feigning interest in the window display of a small shoe shop. From the corner of his eye, he watched Mr N'Dengu turn right at the bottom of the street. Jaydeep ran after him, expecting, when he too turned the corner, to see Mr N'Dengu crossing the road to where the dhows berthed. Instead he headed toward the spice soukh, his height and distinctive lope making him easy to spot in the crowd.

Intrigued, Jaydeep trailed him as he wound his way past the market stalls, each one shrouded in its own olfactory fingerprint. Cinnamon and saffron, frankincense and cardamom tickled his nostrils. It was an enticing reminder that he was in Arabia, which was easy to forget in a city where you spent an inordinate amount of time in American-style mega-malls.

He watched him buy small amounts of colourful spices from a couple of the traders. As Jaydeep himself passed the stalls several metres behind Mr N'Dengu, he briefly inspected the sacks of powder, bending over to smell them. The cinnamon powder looked exactly like the substance in a sealed jar he had seen once in Mr N'Dengu's villa, which was labelled 'powdered hyena spine', while the frankincense looked like something he had spotted in a Perspex box on another shelf labelled, 'tincture of *Crocodylus niloticus*'.

When Mr N'Dengu emerged from a tacky souvenir shop with a dozen onyx camel key-rings, it was the final proof, as if any more were needed that Mr N'Dengu's sorcery skills were a money-grabbing sham. And yet Jaydeep wasn't anywhere near as angry as he thought he would be about this. While they had been conned to the tune of several thousand dirhams, they were, after all, still having a baby. Hadn't a relative once told him that anxiety was the enemy of fertility? Mr N'Dengu's potions had obviously acted as a placebo of sorts. Plus his fee was still a fraction of what the fertility clinic back in the UK would have cost.

And who knows whether that would have worked.

Jaydeep continued to follow his quarry through the congested arteries of the Spice Soukh and into the heart of the Gold Soukh a few streets away. He mingled for a few seconds with a large German tour group as Mr

N'Dengu stopped to light up a cigar in front of a jewellery shop and studied the diamond rings in the window. There had never been, to Jaydeep's knowledge, any mention of a Mrs N'Dengu. Jaydeep was pretty sure he wasn't gay, but then he had felt the same way about his brother, Sachin, too, and he was now happily shacked up with a fireman in Antwerp.

Mr N'Dengu carried on walking through the Gold Soukh and emerged into the busy streets of Naif. Pakistani men in shalwar kameez pulled handcarts piled high with fabrics, as burly Russian gangster types in tight T-shirts shopped with their surly-faced molls. Jaydeep rarely came to this part of town and he was reminded why. Avoiding the pushcarts, keeping an eye on your wallet and avoiding the touts with their 'copyvatches-copyvatches-genuine-fakes' sales spiel, delivered with the verbal dexterity of a rapper, was both physically and mentally exhausting. Feeling his armpits dampen with perspiration, he pined for the relative tranquillity of their street in The Greens.

So it came as a huge relief when Mr N'Dengu slipped into a back-street *shawarma* joint, a restaurant no bigger than a shipping container. From the other side of the road, Jaydeep watched him sit down opposite a slim white woman who was already seated at a table beside the window. The woman was wearing a large straw hat with a blue ribbon around it. Melody had one just like it.

She had Melody's way of sitting, too: prim, with her fingers clasped, resting palms down on the table-top. Jaydeep moved a little closer. Melody had those sunglasses. She had the same dress. Earrings. Pink plastic watch and swallow-tattooed shoulder. The same head, body, heart, mind, DNA. Hell, who was he trying to kid? He'd known it was Melody as soon as he saw her.

He wanted so much to believe that she was meeting Mr N'Dengu to thank him for his services. And maybe he would have had she not reached out just then and held Mr N'Dengu's hand across the table with undeniable affection.

Jaydeep walked down the street, turned into the doorway of a vacant shop, took out his mobile phone with shaking hands and dialled, trying to maintain some semblance of composure.

'Hey, you,' Melody said. 'What's up?'

'Just saying hi,' Jaydeep said. 'So, uh, what are you doing for lunch today?'

'I'm getting a takeaway salad from Wild Peeta.'

'Right,' Jaydeep said.

'Call you back after we've eaten? I'm with… Noura.'

'Cool. Love you.'

'Yeah… You too.'

Jaydeep thought of walking over to the cafe to confront them but he couldn't trust himself to stay calm and refrain from knocking out Mr N'Dengu's perfectly aligned teeth. Maybe he should damage his car in some way. Or vandalise his villa. Each vengeful idea struck him as juvenile, the act of a pissed-off teenager who's just been beaten up by the school bully. Eventually he decided to wait until the following morning and have it out with Melody. Maybe there would be some plausible explanation, but he doubted it. He walked back down the street to where he could see them. She was looking at N'Dengu across that table the way she looked at Jaydeep when they first got together. And back then she didn't have her ardour numbed by St John's fucking Wort and valerian tea.

'The cunt!' Jaydeep said aloud as a teenage Pakistani boy in a shalwar kameez walked by and stared at him.

He reached into his pocket and took out a fifty dirham note and the onyx camel he had been carrying for weeks.

'Hey, my friend,' Jaydeep said to the boy. 'This money is all yours if you give these to that guy in the restaurant over there. Tell him it's from a magic man.'

The boy took the key ring, studied it with mild suspicion, then snatched the note and headed across the street.

Jaydeep was already hailing a cab.

It was 3 a.m. when he finished his shift at the restaurant. It had been a hellish night, his mind crowded with murderous thoughts, not only of Mr N'Dengu, but of three diners who had complained about their food. He had irreparably ruined three tuna steaks and almost sliced off half his pinkie finger while chopping lime leaves for the roast sea bass starter. He had asked Jesse the head chef if he could get off early but it was a Thursday, the night before the weekend. Every table was booked till closing time. 'Don't bother coming back if you walk out that door,' Jesse had said. 'You've been a liability all fucking night.'

He knew something was wrong before he entered their apartment – the building's Nepalese security guard, normally a talkative man, had mumbled a response when he'd wished him goodnight and seemed unable to look him in the eye. The first sign that Melody had left him was the brown envelope bearing his name that was lying on the kitchen table beneath the onyx camel. He took the envelope and opened it. Inside was a sheet of paper on which was written: *We've left the country. So sorry it ended this way. I'll explain some day. M.*

Jaydeep ran into the bedroom, looked in all the wardrobes and cupboards, but Melody had taken nearly everything that was hers, and a few things that weren't – like the expensive watch she had bought him for their second wedding anniversary and their shared iPad. He went into the nursery room but that was intact, its contents too big to fit into a getaway suitcase. Her passport had been taken.

He tried calling Melody's mobile but it was switched off.

He thought about calling the police to report Mr N'Dengu as a sorcerer, an offence punishable by law, but realised that they might come around the apartment to ask him questions. At least one cupboard in his kitchen was filled with alcohol and he would have to dispose of it first as he didn't have the required liquor license.

He'd also have to admit that he had used Mr N'Dengu's services, which was probably an offence too. And in any case, he wanted answers far more than he wanted revenge. He needed to know if the baby was his. If there was a baby at all. He had taken her word for it and had seen no real evidence. He wanted to know whether she really wanted to run off and make a new life with a cheap conman. What could Mr N'Dengu offer her that he couldn't?

He realised there was a chance they hadn't left yet, that they were still packing up in the villa in Umm Suqeim.

Jaydeep got into his car and drove there as fast as the traffic allowed.

Nobody answered the doorbell when he rang it. Shaking the rungs of the gate, the pink-feathered contraption now looking more like something a dancer would wear at *The Folies Bergère* than a repellant of evil, he shouted first Melody's name then Zeema's. Eventually a neighbour, a grey-haired Scottish man with a dog, came along and asked if he could help.

'Do you know where they've gone?' Jaydeep said.

'I believe they left this evening,' the man said. 'Mr N'Dengu, his mother and some other woman he's been knocking around with lately. Pretty thing.'

'Right. It's just... well, I wanted to give him something before he left.'

'Well, Gambia, I think he said he was going. Or is it Zambia? Might even be Zaire. His business was in a bit of trouble apparently. Wasn't in his interests to stay in Dubai. He thought all that furniture made by African tribesmen would sell here. Didn't work out by all accounts. Gave me a nice table before he left, though. Can't say the missus is too pleased, being an animal lover, but it was generous of him.'

'Yes, very generous,' Jaydeep said through gritted teeth.

'Funny thing is, I didn't know what he did until today. Kept himself to himself since he moved in about six months ago. I don't want to sound like a bigot but I thought he might have been a drug dealer at one point. People coming and going at strange hours. That fancy car of his. Plenty of good-looking lasses.'

As the man broke off to scoop up some freshly laid dog shit, Jaydeep got into his car and headed for the airport. He wanted to be absolutely sure they had left the country.

It didn't take him long to find Mr N'Dengu's silver Audi. When he looked through the window he saw that the electronic smart key had been left on the driver's seat. Another car relinquished by absconders who had gotten into debt or fallen foul of the law. Rumour had it the airport car park was replenished with such vehicles on a weekly basis since the economic fall-out.

Jaydeep opened the door and sat in the passenger seat where Melody must have been sitting only hours, maybe minutes before. A glass evil-eye amulet dangled from the rear-view mirror. Catching the faintest whiff of Melody's favourite perfume, he ran his fingers along the dashboard in front of him, imagining her fingers there too. He turned on the engine and the song that boomed out from the speakers was the same one Jaydeep had heard Mr N'Dengu play that day on his way to the Soukh. 'Running Away' by Roy Ayers. Very fucking ironic.

He pressed eject and the CD it spewed out had his very own handwriting on it. 'Jaydeep's Funky Fifteen Pt.3'. It was a compilation he had made for Melody about a year ago for the long journey to an acting workshop she had to attend in Liwa. She had been involved in a minor car accident on the way back and he had driven out to a desert village three hours away to help her sort it out with the young Emirati couple who had been in the other car. They had ended up spending the night at the other couple's villa playing with their 18-month-old twins, a heart-meltingly cute boy and a girl. The woman had asked Melody why they had no children of their own and when Melody said they were trying, the woman had said, 'Inshallah, next year you will be with a child.'

Jaydeep brought his fist down on the middle of the steering wheel. 'FUCKING BITCH!' He surprised himself by wiping away a tear. He couldn't remember the last time he cried and wondered whether he was more upset by the shame of being cuckolded than the disappointment of learning he probably wasn't going to be a father.

Thinking he might find some clues as to where they were heading, he opened the glove compartment. Inside were two pairs of sunglasses, a half-smoked cigar, and a bundle of papers and envelopes. He shuffled through them. Some of them were e-tickets for flights to India. Others were receipts and documents for business transactions he didn't understand. But the same place and name kept cropping up. A Dr Rakesh K. Murthy who appeared to run some sort of medical centre in Calcutta.

The first thing he did when he got home was type 'Rakesh K. Murthy, Calcutta' into Google. There were 7,462 hits but the first hundred or so were newspaper articles all related to the same topic. Jaydeep had only to read a couple before the penny dropped. Murthy, a smug-looking middle-aged man with a penchant for cravats and a Poirot-style moustache, ran a controversial IVF clinic that helped wealthy Indian women get pregnant with designer sperm, donated by men with allegedly superior physical attributes. Jaydeep, six feet two, athletic, university educated and light-skinned on account of his Bengali father and an English mother, was just the kind of biological father these high-caste women sought to procreate with, if not in the intimate way.

He stood up and ambled, drunk on confusion, to the nursery. Switching on the light he collapsed backwards into the mini-mountain of fluffy toys he had been accumulating since the day Melody had told him she was pregnant. When everything in his world had seemed to align itself. When his life suddenly had a single, vital purpose. Earlier today it had been snatched away, and now, before the reality of that could sink in, it was as if his world was on the move again, like it had found an extra gear and was hurtling at a pace too fast to cling on to.

He thought about the seeds of his loin being dispersed like a dandelion's across India. He envisioned strands of his DNA spreading like railtracks across a continent and beyond, weeks, years, centuries from now, just like Ghenghis Khan's.

He sank further into the pile of toys, pulling them over him until they covered him completely. He was going to be a father a thousand times over and in a country as big as India he could spend his whole life tracing the children that were his. He could go insane with the ineffable vastness of it.

He got up and walked into the kitchen and poured

himself a triple-shot of the finest whisky he had. Then he went out on to the veranda of their villa and raised his glass to the crescent moon and stars that had come out to greet him on a still winter night.

The Sound Between

Three a.m. and I'm partying in a mansion that Hugh Hefner would deem decadent. Driveway flanked by rearing bronze stallions. Fountains on the front lawn that make Trafalgar Square look like a graveyard for burst water hydrants. And marble. Lots and lots of marble. We could be in Beverly Hills were it not for the green minarets across the street that stand like giant asparagus spears beside the bulbous dome of a mosque.

In the main room a DJ with braided hair and bad jewellery stands hunched over the turntables, his brow furrowed with concentration, as though he's shaping something on a potter's wheel. He plays 'Good Life' by Inner City, 'Livin' It Up' by Jah Rule. Feel-good anthems that form the soundtrack to our gilt-edged lives.

Out in the high-walled garden there is a large oval swimming pool with a black dollar-sign mosaic on its floor. It undulates beneath the ripples made by drunken, half-naked people having a water fight. I want the water to win. United in their smugness they drink from fishbowl glasses filled with cocktails and chlorine.

Abhishek, my work colleague who has dragged me here tonight, mentions in his refined Indian accent something about this being the 'quintessential' Dubai crowd. Emirates cabin crew, free of their staid uniforms and red pill-box hats, tastefully flash the flesh in designer frocks. Behind an apple-scented veil of sheesha smoke and humidity, a group of hair-gelled film industry types from the Levant discuss the tumultuous events in Egypt and Syria. Dangling their skinny ankles into the swimming pool, a trio of off-duty Filipina waitresses giggle amongst themselves, no doubt grateful to the plump German friend of the host who has handed them the ticket to this other world. Westerners make up the rest of the throng, from brawny South African surf instructors to English-toff investment bankers in pastel-coloured polo shirts, a paragon of good behaviour until they have that one drink too many and someone spills the dregs of a bellini over their Tod's suede loafers. Exactly where I, a low-ranking advertising copywriter, fit into all this is reassuringly uncertain.

Watching me observe the crowd, Abhishek taps me on the elbow and says, 'Isn't this fucking *awesome*, man? We'll tell our children about nights like these. These are boom-times, you know? Like… like New York in the twenties when it started erecting skyscrapers the way a refugee camp puts up tents.'

I smile and remind him about 2008 when Dubai hit the skids, not that I was here then, but he tells me to stop dwelling on the past and live in the moment, snatches a champagne bottle off a passing guest and fills my glass to the brim. 'Drink up,' he demands, jerking his thumb towards the cabin crew girls. 'I'm feeling lucky.'

It's not that I'm ungrateful for these regular Friday night parties at swanky villas and penthouse apartments, but before moving to Dubai I had expected a modesty and restraint that was in short supply in the media maelstrom of London. So easy to get caught up in it all: the private members bars, guest-list places at clubs where footballers and actors banged fake-titted glamour models two at a time in the toilets, the pressure from colleagues to have another line.

After five years of bacchanalian excess I was looking forward to downsizing my decadence. New faces and places beckoned. My weary body craved respite from the endless waves of recreational abuse. Goodbye cocaine and awkward breakfasts with nameless women. Hello weekend walks on the beach, scuba diving off the Omani coast, and slow winding drives through the desert as the sun's golden rays warmed the soft-top of my Jeep Wrangler. Dubai was no Riyadh, joyless and oppressive, I knew that. But I never expected to gain access to this world with such ease. I thought it was reserved for Arab playboys and their sycophantic minions.

I'm musing upon the madness, the baffling contradictions of this city, when suddenly, as if God himself has had enough, there's a blackout, and the song that is playing – that old classic, 'Groove Is In The Heart' by Deee-Lite – ends abruptly.

'FUGGIN' POWER CUT!' shouts Hossein, our pony-tailed Persian host, as he stomps off into another room, presumably to find a torch.

Little squares of light from mobile phones emerge like fat fireflies in the darkness. There are peals of confused laughter, the smash of a glass, splashes from the pool. We stand around, waiting for the beat to pound from the speakers again. Seconds turn into minutes and we start to think that maybe the pulse really has gone out of the party and it's time to leave.

Then it begins.

A sound, not from the speakers, but from some place beyond the garden walls. It is deep – somber in tone – and I recognise it eventually as the noise that has woken me up each morning since I arrived in Dubai. The Muezzin from the nearby mosque. I don't understand any of it, this half-sung, half-spoken call to prayer. But suddenly it feels wrong to be standing here knocking back five-hundred-dirham-a-bottle Verve Clicquot; even if the pretty blonde next to me seems oblivious as she shows me the jewel-festooned Cartier wristwatch she's just been given by her French-Lebanese boyfriend.

Eventually the lights come back on, but the music doesn't. I look across at the DJ who is flicking through his box of tunes, dots of red lights on his mixing desk blinking to life. I glance at surrounding faces and I know that everyone else is listening to the Muezzin too because nobody is talking.

I watch the DJ choose a CD and insert it into the player and my mind goes blank as I find myself thinking: how do you follow a prayer?

Not with reggae or seventies jazz funk. Not with thumping techno or Lady Gaga. Not even with Mozart or Mahler.

The DJ's head is bowed and he stands very still, as though he's observing a minute's silence on Remembrance Sunday. I'm pleased that he at least has the decency to wait until the Muezzin finishes, his voice slipping out of earshot like a whisper in the wind. But then, as if there really is no other option than to get the party started again, he leans his braided head over his mixing console, slides across the fader and flicks a switch. The beat kicks in and – horror of horrors – it's Kanye West or Snoop Dogg, or one of those other jewel-toothed guys who rap about bitches and niggaz and motherfuckin' hoes.

The sacrilege of the act goes unacknowledged and the party continues as if nothing has happened. Abhishek, fully-clothed and still clutching the bottle of champagne, jumps into the pool with the three Filipinas while a grinning fat bald guy in a Barcelona football shirt films them on his mobile phone. Two girls on the makeshift dance floor wearing rubber-rings around their midriffs playfully bump into one of their friends who wobbles on precariously lofty heels.

Hossein, standing at one end of the pool with a cigar in his mouth and his hands on his hips, surveys the scene with the unmistakable satisfaction of a restaurant owner seeing his establishment full to capacity on opening night.

Feeling tired and drowsy from the alcohol I decide to call it quits, so I finish my drink and try to call a taxi, but the operator can't hear me over the music. Nobody sees me as I let myself out of the garden via a side door and walk into the street. The operator says there won't be any cars available for at least half an hour, maybe longer, but I order one anyway. When I try to get back into the garden, however, no one hears me banging the door. I call Abhishek's mobile but he doesn't answer. Behind the wall, the party continues without me. In a small, unlit alleyway halfway along the street I sit down in the soft sand, my back pressed against the wall. I fall asleep while waiting for the taxi driver to arrive and when I wake up a few hours later, the harsh brilliance of the morning light stings my eyes. When I'm able to focus properly, I see the minarets of the mosque looming over me in silhouette and the events of the previous night come flooding back. I stand up, dust myself off and head home, determined not to forget them.

Zeina

After a while, we noticed that Zeina had begun to shed her clothing like a stripper working in instalments. The non-Muslims joked quietly amongst themselves that she would be in hotpants by Ramadan.

During her first weeks at the *Gazette* she had worn a loose-fitting black *abaya*, only her face, hands and a few rogue strands of hair on show. Since moving to Dubai two months earlier I had grown used to the sight of similarly dressed Emirati women in the shopping malls, a gust of olfactory opulence trailing them as they ghosted by, *kohl*-eyed and straight-backed, the train of their *abayas* sweeping pristine marble floors. Peeking out from the black folds of cloth, you might glimpse a shiny Manolo Blahnik heel, or the stellar glint of a diamond-encrusted bangle. We asked Western female acquaintances, less out of prurience than curiosity, what they saw underneath when in the washrooms. The answer: $300 jeans, jewellery worthy of Cleopatra and expensively pampered skin.

We lapped up these revelations, certain we would never get a sniff of the Emirati women ourselves. They were too virtuous for casual flings with roving-eyed expats – haughty some said – but mostly they were simply, unapproachably beautiful, just like Zeina. And yet soon after she began working as a photographer on the newsdesk, her gradual unwrapping hinted at a girl who followed the rigours of her culture and religion with less zeal than her Emirati sisters.

One morning, about a month after she started, Zeina caused a stir at the office by turning up with her head exposed for the first time. She looked more striking than ever with her blue-black hair cascading down her back, her *abaya* hugging the contours of her body. Many of her female colleagues came from other, more liberal Middle Eastern countries – Lebanon, Egypt, Jordan – and wore Western dress. We assumed she was taking her sartorial cue from them.

By her third month Zeina appeared to have renounced traditional dress completely, turning up in loose-fitting trousers and long-sleeved tops. Shortly after that, she seemed to have reached a terminus: demure skirts that stalled chastely below the knee, sensible shoes, and blouses that barely revealed her collarbone let alone the inverted V of cleavage proffered by some of the other women in the office. Emboldened by her change in appearance and learning that Zeina was unmarried at twenty-six, some of the guys began to talk in hushed tones of asking her out on a date.

Frank Dano, a sports reporter from Sydney who more than lived up to his first name, overheard us talking in the canteen one lunchtime. 'Fine for their men to fuck our women,' he said, practically foaming at the mouth 'but lay a finger on theirs and you can cop a shitload of strife.' You had to admit that Frank had a point. To go out with Zeina would be taboo to say the least, and I doubted anyone would even try. Sure enough, six months after she had joined the company, even Terry Lowe in sales, a lecherous divorcee and incorrigible purveyor of bullshit who preyed on the city's abundant supply of air hostesses, hadn't dared approach her.

As a photographer, Zeina went out on assignments alone or with a female reporter. Such gender-dividing arrangements were not uncommon in the Gulf workplace and Conrad, the editor-in-chief, accepted them grudgingly. But when things got really hectic, she would have no choice but to team up with a male reporter like myself. Zeina had her own car, though, and would always travel alone to the location of her assignment.

One stiflingly hot day in late August, I was sent to interview an American movie producer who was shooting a film in the Hatta mountains. I was pleased to discover that Zeina would be the accompanying photographer. Although we had exchanged greetings in the corridors at work and I had once sat next to her at a staff meeting held in the boardroom, we had never spoken at length.

The interview took place in a Venetian-themed cafe at the hotel where the producer was staying. I arrived first and, as planned, Zeina turned up when I was about halfway through. She sat at a table designed to look like a gondola on the opposite side of the room, preparing her equipment as I chatted to the producer, a thick-set man in a brown pinstripe suit who jigged his knee and responded to every question with a look of incredulity, as though I had asked him which of his children he would save first if his house was on fire. Worse, he insisted throughout the interview on calling me 'kid'.

Noticing Zeina, he beckoned me closer. 'That lil honey back there,' he whispered, jerking his head in her direction. 'She's your snapper, right?'

I nodded.

He could hardly take his eyes off her. The interview, clearly, was over.

Finishing my coffee, I watched Zeina confidently shepherd the producer around the cafe, coaxing him into a number of different poses. I cringed when he offered her a cigarette out of an ornate silver case.

'Thank you, no, it is *haram*,' she said, forcing a smile. 'Forbidden.'

'You don't mind if I do, right?' the producer said, lighting one for himself.

Afterwards, Zeina and I left the hotel together and waited for the valets to bring our cars. Mine came first. When I saw that it had a flat tyre I almost swore out loud; I had used my spare on a trip to Oman the previous month.

'Too bad, Scott,' said Zeina. 'A taxi will come soon, *inshallah*.'

Her car arrived seconds later – a yellow four-wheel-drive with tinted windows – and I watched as she put her equipment into the boot. Then she drove off down the street, leaving me standing there in the heat, my shirt already freckling with sweat. I tried not to feel irritated and reminded myself that this was nothing personal, just the way things were done here. I had no time for British colleagues who complained that the cultural and social codes didn't emulate those of their own country. These were the sort of people who spent their weekends propping up the bars of theme pubs, refused to learn a single word of Arabic and whinged every year about the nightclubs closing for Ramadan. I gave them a wide berth, preferring to spend my time with a bunch of friendly Spaniards who lived in my apartment block. My colleagues considered me square, aloof even, but I didn't care. I wanted more out of Dubai than a beer gut and a suntan.

I was about to go back into the hotel to call a cab when Zeina's four-wheel-drive reappeared from around the block, a muffled dance beat thumping from within. It stopped abruptly in front of me and the driver's side window lowered a couple of inches. Zeina's *kohl*-rimmed eyes looked out from the gap.

'*Yalla*,' she said. 'Come, I will take you.'

Sitting in the passenger seat next to Zeina, I felt tongue-tied, anxious not to make a *faux pas* like the film producer. It was rush hour by now and the city's roads bulged with traffic. Cars – from brand new Ferraris to rusty Toyotas – spilled onto the hard shoulder and grey fumes spewed from exhaust pipes like lit cigarettes. Up ahead of us a bus filled with tired-looking Indian workers had broken down, blocking the middle lane and sparking a cacophony of frustrated beeps.

Zeina sighed, gesturing at the traffic, and switched off the American R&B that was thumping out of the stereo. The silence exacerbated my unease. A loop of prayer beads – I was surprised by this religious paraphernalia – hung from the rear-view mirror and rapped the windscreen each time her foot touched the brake, which was often in that stop-start traffic.

Finally we reached Sheikh Zayed Road, five-star hotels lining each side, forming a long corridor of architectural splendour. I must have driven down it a thousand times over, but it never failed to cast a hypnotic spell over me.

'Scott?' said Zeina, snapping her fingers inches from my face. Painted on her right hand was an intricate web of henna that disappeared into the cuff of her white blouse. Images – an apple, a keyhole – emerged in the pattern, like shifting clouds.

She gave a short laugh. 'For a moment I thought you had fallen asleep.'

'Just admiring the scenery,' I said.

'Seems like a new building appears here every day, huh?' said Zeina. 'The old Dubai… it's disappearing in more ways than one.' She said this, I thought, with none of the regret or nostalgia with which I had heard older Emiratis say the same thing.

As she fixed her eyes on the road ahead I glanced at her in profile. The arms of the chunky white Gucci sunglasses she wore inside and outside the office – a kind of trademark – stood out against her flawless brown skin. Catching a glimpse of my unshaven face in the mirror above the prayer beads, I wished I had been given forewarning of our assignment so I could have made myself more presentable. I felt self-consciously unkempt in her presence, which was never less than immaculate.

I rubbed my eyes, more out of tiredness than the glare of the sun. When I opened them, Zeina had removed her sunglasses.

'Here' she said, dropping them into my lap. I didn't really need them but something made me accept.

'*Shukran*,' I said.

'*Afwan.*'

We giggled as I put on the sunglasses and checked my reflection in the mirror. I could smell Zeina's perfume on the plastic, that unmistakable scent of incense, dense as humidity.

'They suit you, Scott,' she said. 'You look pretty cool.'

'They suit *you* better,' I said, but I kept them on. I was enjoying their light aroma, breathing it in like the smell of something good on the stove.

'A present… from someone I used to know,' she said.

'An ex-boyfriend?' I wanted so much to say those words, and for a brief moment it seemed as though she might elaborate, unprompted. But then her expression grew tight and she distracted herself by needlessly fiddling with the air-conditioning switch.

Eventually, the traffic eased off and we were approaching the office, a pale blue three-storey building on an industrial estate shrouded in dust.

About fifty metres away from the staff car park, Zeina pulled up to the side of the road and jerked up the handbrake. It took a second to realise that she expected me to get out.

She shrugged her shoulders. 'It's my culture. Otherwise we... I'm sorry.'

I removed my seatbelt. 'You don't have to explain,' I said. 'I might even make my deadline, thanks to you.'

I stood outside the car for what seemed like ages, holding the door open, trying to think of the right thing to say, something... I don't know, memorable, witty. Something to make her want to spend more time with me.

Pathetically, I ended up simply thanking her for the lift.

'You're welcome. *Afwan*,' she said, before breaking into a big smile, and I wondered whether it was from the relief of offloading me, her forbidden cargo, or whether I had done enough to win her affection.

I shut the door and she pulled away. Through the darkened glass I caught the movement of an arm, obscured by the flapping of an open shirt cuff. Corny as it sounds, I like to think she blew me a kiss.

By the time I got to the entrance Zeina was already inside chatting to the receptionist. Then Terry Lowe popped out of the revolving doors, as if they were the exit point on a factory assembly line that manufactured wankers.

'Scottyboy!' he said, blocking my way and twirling his car keys around his middle finger. 'Lovin' the shades, mate. Very Jackie-O.'

Reflexively, I brought my hands up to my eyes, felt the smooth, hard plastic of Zeina's sunglasses. Cursing my carelessness, I snatched them off, and stuffed them into my bag.

Terry moved aside, about to walk away, when he suddenly swivelled around to look back into the reception area. When he turned around to face me again he was grinning.

'My *maaan*!' he said, walking backwards towards his car. He was pointing at me, a gun-shape formed by his thumb and forefinger. 'Careful those ragheads don't catch you messin' with that.'

I wanted to punch him, wanted to see his blood blacken the sand between our feet.

'Secret's safe with me,' he said. 'Safe as houses.'

Grinning still, he ducked into his convertible and wheel-spun away. The article on the film producer came out the next day, the worst thing I have ever written and memorable for one thing only: the smitten look on the producer's face in the accompanying photographs.

Aim High, Olongapo

Watching from the bathroom window, I wait until their car has turned the corner at the end of the driveway then go downstairs to the *majlis* where Mr Matoush hides the key for his study. Through the holes in my flip-flops the cold floor tiles surprise the soles of my feet. The air conditioning is always on in here. It is refreshing, like being in the frozen food aisle at a supermarket, whereas my own room in the basement is so hot that each morning I have to banana-peel my sticky nightdress off my skin.

I take the key from beneath the jewelled box and head toward the front of the house, checking on Nabeela as I pass her room. Lying in her crib, she plays with a fluffy toy, watching me with huge brown eyes as round as coins. She will grow up, I think, to be as beautiful as her mother, a timid and kind woman who is far too good for a man as bad-tempered as her husband.

In Mr Matoush's study the smell of incense tickles my nostrils. He burns it most days in a little clay pot on his desk, the pale blue smoke filling the house and clinging to every fabric surface. For Nabeela especially, this is not healthy. But then what right have I, a maid, to protest about such things?

I switch on the computer – it takes a minute or so to come to life – and look up at the clock on the wall.

I have so little time.

Today is my daughter's third birthday. Her name is Angel Constantina Abalos and she is the reason I am a million miles away from our home in Olongapo in the Philippines, the reason I change the diapers of a baby that is not mine, wash and iron the clothes of a man who is not my husband, and scrub the floors of a home that is as different from my tiny house in Olongapo as a cathedral to a phone booth.

Each night, before I roll out the rubber mattress I have been given to sleep on, I pray that one day she will understand why I could not always be with her on such important days, and that she will love me for the sacrifices I have made, not hate me for the absence that has so far clouded her life. This job pays for her education, new clothes and the never-ending medical bills, but when I watch Mrs Matoush wet Nabeela's head with kisses, breastfeed her, take long evening baths with her, I feel hopeless. What kind of mother am I, I ask myself, who must demonstrate her love through wires and plastic from the other side of the world?

The computer requires no password, so I log straight on to Skype. Mr Matoush uses it most days to keep in touch with his brother, Salim, a student at a university in Beirut, but I have found a way to set up my own account without him knowing.

I make sure the webcam is pointing at me. I can't wait to see my daughter's smile, see the neat rows of baby teeth that now crowd her tiny pink mouth. I make the call, then sit back and wait, hoping my husband Eduardo is already at the house of my brother Soy who owns a computer.

Two minutes pass without reply.

We arranged this only last week. Surely he has not forgotten. Has he remembered the time difference? It is only eight o'clock in Dubai but midnight in the Philippines. Angel will be tired after spending the day playing with her birthday gifts – gifts paid for out of the money I send home each month. So it seems unfair that it is me who must settle for the scraps of her day, those moments before bedtime when she becomes irritable and her bottom lip starts to stick out. Eduardo, the family joker, calls it her 'grumpy goldfish' face.

Looking out of the window, I glance at the big metal gate at the bottom of the drive-way, and then again at the clock, wishing I had the power to freeze time with a click of the mouse. If he knew I was in his study, Mr Matoush would beat me and deduct money from my salary. Three months ago, when Angel was sick, I begged to return home for two weeks. This made him so furious that he punched me in the arm and ripped up my passport. Since then I have been forbidden to leave the house alone and am permitted to communicate with my family only by phone calls, which I must make in the presence of Mr Matoush.

Eduardo has asked me why I speak to him in English, rather than Tagalog. I told him that I do so out of courtesy, but in truth, Mr Matoush insists upon it so I cannot speak ill of him or tell anyone the reality of my life here. But he need not worry about that. Eduardo has enough problems looking after our daughter and holding down his job driving a jeepney without me adding to his burdens. Besides, what could he do, being so far away?

At last, I see movement on the screen. It is Eduardo, his round face filling the frame as he leans forward to position the webcam. The picture is fuzzy and his movements are jerky. He is clean-shaven, his hair neatly parted in the middle and glossy with oil, as if he is about to go to church. Since the last time I saw him the pouches of skin under his eyes seem to have drooped further down his face, making him look more and more like his father. It makes me wonder who really suffers most from this situation – Angel, Eduardo or me?

Eduardo turns to his left and calls our daughter from another room. She comes into view, waddling like a little duck, and Eduardo lifts her on to his lap. By the strain on his face, either he has grown weaker or Angel is getting heavier, maybe from the candy he spoils her with. She has her thumb in her mouth and wears a silver tiara and plastic angel wings. Eduardo points me out on the screen and when she sees me she smiles her new smile and reaches out, her arms opening wide, hungry for the warmth of my embrace.Without really thinking, I stroke the screen, trying to remember the feel of her hair wound around my finger, the smell of papaya soap and baby lotion on her skin. As always, she looks confused, as if her silly mother has shrunk and fallen into a plastic box. Sometimes I think I have become as unreal to her as a character from a TV show. It is a thought that hurts me far more than any punch from Yasser Matoush.

'*Maligayang kaarawan anak!*' I say. 'Happy Birthday, Cutie-pie. You look so beautiful. Did you have a nice day?'

Eduardo says that she did, and lists all the wonderful things they have done. Shopping at the mall, lunch at Jollibee, blowing the candles out on her cake, and the evening party at Soy's with the balloons and candy and ice cream. 'Hey, not too much candy, Eddo,' I say. 'A growing child needs mangoes and milk.'

I ask for other news. Of my sister Gina's new baby, Soy's latest girlfriend and whether Manny Pacquiao will get dragged down by the politics of our country or stick to what he knows best and win his next fight against a Puerto Rican who has knocked out four of his last twelve opponents.

Eduardo tells me about the big new sign '**AIM HIGH, OLONGAPO**' that has been put up beside the road into town. 'It was painted by children from a local school,' he says, 'and is as colourful as a coral reef and as big as a bus.' This fills my mind with good thoughts, makes me think of my *kabayans* back home: the teenagers on the basketball court who play until their angry fathers call them home, the *tanbays* drinking bottled beer on the crowded sidewalks, and our noisy neighbours the Romeros, who have six skinny sons whose names begin with M. I have never seen Mr or Mrs Matoush speak to *any* of their neighbours. This I find strange and sad.

47

My tears have stopped now, held back by the pride I feel for my home, Olongapo, where my roots run deep, where my heart beats loudest.

It is almost nine o'clock so I tell Eduardo that Mr Matoush needs to use the computer and that I have to go.

'It's your daughter's birthday, Deena,' he says. 'Ask him, please, for just five more minutes. Let me speak to him.'

'No. He is a very busy man,' I say.

'But not a kind man?' asks Eduardo.

No, I want to say. A hateful man. A heartless man who curses and pulls my hair until it falls out in clumps. A man who refuses to let me go to my daughter when she is sick. I feel my fists clench, a scream of helplessness seeking some escape from my beaten body. But somehow I compose myself, hold my tongue once more. I will not pile additional pressure on Eduardo, who had so many concerns about me coming to this country in the first place.

'I'll be in touch again soon,' I tell him. 'I promise.'

'Are you *really* okay, Deena?' Eduardo says, quietly. 'If you want to quit this job you can. It's okay. We will get by somehow.'

'I am fine,' I say. 'This will not be forever – just a few more years, a few more pesos to buy the *sari-sari* store we've talked about for our future.'

'And Mr Matoush will have no problem?'

'There will be no problem,' I tell him. 'When Nabeela is old enough to start school, before Angel's tenth birthday, he has said I may leave if I wish.'

Eduardo nods his head and mumbles something about me doing whatever I think is best. Then we all say our goodbyes and I love yous and I switch off the computer and leave the study, remembering to lock the door and return the key exactly as I found it to the box in the *majlis*.

I go into Nabeela's room and see that she is still awake, so I scoop her up and carry her into the parlour. Cradling her in my arms, I hum a lullaby I used to sing to Angel when she was a baby. I close my eyes and try to pretend this little bundle is my own flesh and blood; but it is no good. She does not smell the same, does not sound the same. Even the way she moves – her tiny legs pedalling the air with her chubby knees pointing east and west – is different.

By the time I see car headlights glowing on the driveway several minutes later Nabeela is back in her crib, asleep, and I am preparing supper in the kitchen, chopping onions so that I have a reason for my sore red eyes.

Pictures in the Dust

It was around midday when the Indian man in the grubby blue overalls walked into the gallery, sand spilling from his work boots and sullying the white-tiled floor. The heat chased him through the door and a waft of hot air reached Laird who looked up from his desk and fanned himself with a magazine.

The man, who had a spade-shaped nose and an elaborate moustache, smiled shyly at Laird, then began to pass along the paintings that lined the walls, his clumpy boots at odds with his wiry frame.

Laird could tell from the man's overalls that he was a labourer, probably from the construction site next door where they were laying the foundations of a new apartment block. Sometimes Laird, venturing outside, would find a dozen of them lying around the back of the gallery as they sought refuge on their lunch break from the scorching Gulf sun. Sprawled out on strips of cardboard, they slept with their boots off, the blue mass of bodies emitting a susurration of gentle snores that could be heard across the street. Faint smiles, induced by dreams of home or the pleasure of having their blistered feet caressed by the breeze, played on their sun-withered faces.

Laird turned a blind eye to their presence so long as they stayed around the back where they weren't obstructing customers. Occasionally he brought them tea and biscuits and gave them old shirts he no longer wore. Like everyone, he knew of their meagre wages, their squalid living conditions in Sonapur and other overcrowded camps on the outskirts of the city where tourists never strayed. It was their blood and sweat that had built this metropolis out of the sand and it angered Laird to see them treated with a contempt reserved for lepers.

The man was now standing close by as he studied one of the paintings, a dreary watercolour of some sand dunes by a locally-based artist for which the gallery owner, Mahmoud, had an inexplicable soft spot. There was no point offering the man assistance, Laird mused; he looked in no position to buy even the cheapest exhibit. Pretending to read his magazine, Laird watched him tweak his moustache, the ends of which doubled back on themselves, threatening to thread through the needle-eyes of his nostrils. His slender fingers and the smooth skin on his hands belied his profession – the pair of cement-speckled gloves hanging out of his back pocket evidently served their purpose.

'Like that painting, do you?' asked Laird, intrigued.

He hadn't had a customer for hours and was glad of the opportunity to exercise his vocal chords.

The man was about to reply when a flurry of raps rained on the glass of the gallery's front window. A fat, dark-skinned man in a yellow hard-hat and a shirt and tie stood on the pavement outside tapping his watch.

'Your boss?' asked Laird.

The man waggled his head before dashing out of the gallery, leaving a trail of sand in his wake.

A ray of sun reflected off the chrome handle of the door as it slowly swung shut behind him. It swept across the floor of the gallery in a lighthouse beam. For a brief moment, it made the sand on the tiles sparkle like gold dust.

The following week Laird was locking up the gallery for the day, when he saw Mahmoud hurrying back towards the building. He had left only seconds earlier in a huff, having had a minor disagreement with Laird about taking on the work of a new artist, a man who painted villas and swimming pools in a style that shamelessly mimicked David Hockney.

'Come, quickly,' Mahmoud said, opening the gallery door and beckoning Laird to follow him. 'You won't believe this.'

They walked to a large expanse of sand behind the gallery that was used as a parking lot. When they got to Laird's old white saloon, his first thought was that it had been vandalised. A picture of a lion's head, its mouth agape, teeth like sabers, covered every inch of the bonnet.

Mahmoud licked his forefinger and ran it through the lion's mane. He raised the digit as if testing the direction of the wind. It was then that Laird realised that the image was rendered not in paint, as he had first thought, but in the thick layer of ochre dust that coated the vehicle because he hadn't cleaned it in so long. It was so lifelike that he felt as if he could insert his hand deep into the lion's cave of a mouth, feel on his face its hot, carnivorous breath.

Mahmoud stood with his hands on his hips, shaking his head in disbelief.

'Now *that's* talent,' he said. 'We should get it photographed.'

Laird laughed. 'It can't stay there. I'm getting it cleaned tomorrow.'

When Laird drove through the carwash the following day, he felt a tinge of regret as the image rinsed away before his eyes.

During the following months, several more pictures were found etched into the grimy surface of Laird's saloon. There was the brace of snakes that wrapped themselves almost around the whole car; bloated go-faster stripes. A drooping palm tree flanked by little pyramids of fallen coconuts on one of the back passenger doors and, no less spectacular because of its dinkier proportions, a cavalcade of camels that formed a thin frieze along the top of the windscreen. One day, when he was looking down onto the roof of the vehicle from the balcony of his apartment, he saw a Spanish galleon sailing on stormy seas. Peering down to inspect it he could have sworn he saw the ship list slightly, the water swell beneath it, but he put it down to a trick of the light, a mirage. Each picture was drawn in such intricate detail that it seemed to conjure that effect; this spooked and fascinated Laird in equal measure.

He felt that somehow each picture was a kind of talisman protecting his car from danger and, to Laird's delight, the worst of the city's traffic congestion. Several times he had narrowly escaped collisions on the city's highways, and every red light he hit changed instantly to green. On one trip he had made to a client in a remote village in Liwa – shortly after discovering a beautiful picture of an orchid on his bonnet – he found he had underestimated the length of the journey and was convinced he was going to run out of gas in the middle of the desert. He watched as the needle hovered above the red until he found a petrol station after seventy anxious kilometres.

Intrigued, Laird began to encourage the mystery artist, allowing a thick patina of dust to build up on his car. After the yearly *shamal* winds had whipped around the city, depositing a thin layer of sand on everything in sight, he must have been the only driver not to rush to the nearest carwash.

At the end of each working day he felt buoyed with anticipation as he walked from the gallery to the car park. A whole month might go by – and nothing. Then there would be two, maybe three pictures in one week. Only on Laird's car, though, never on any of the other vehicles that were parked nearby.

His curiosity at bursting point, Laird began to park his car closer and closer to the gallery, watching it from the window as though it were parked in a street of thieves.

Then one lunchtime, on his way to the cafe down the street, he stopped in his tracks. The man had his back to him and was on his haunches, bare feet perched on the edge of the bonnet as he worked. As he got closer, the sand cushioning his footsteps, Laird saw the gloves hanging from the back pocket of the man's blue overalls.

Laird coughed, startling the man, who leapt to the ground. Realising he wasn't about to be scolded, he beamed with pride, looking back at his work in progress – a leaping marlin – then back at Laird, raising his eyebrows as if awaiting affirmation of his talent, a Roman emperor-style thumbs-up.

Urging him to carry on, Laird watched the man work, watched him use the different parts of his hands and fingers the way a painter uses different sized brushes. He was as deft with his digits as a conjuror of coins. When he finished, he climbed down off the car, grinning, and took a theatrical bow.

Using a mixture of English and some Hindi he had picked up on a gap-year travelling around India, Laird asked him to drop by the gallery later in the week. He tried to explain that maybe he could help him get work through his many contacts – as an illustrator, perhaps, or a painter of murals in the mansions of the wealthy Arab businessmen who patronised the gallery. He hadn't been so excited about an artist for years. This man was probably self-taught, never set foot in art college. And as for that stealthy way of working, Laird thought he could turn out to be Dubai's answer to Banksy. Perhaps a year from now he would be unveiled to the world, becoming a superstar with a multi-million dollar book deal.

Seeing his colleagues rising and tugging on their boots, the man indicated that he had to return to work.

'Badlu,' he said, smiling and tapping his chest.

'Laird,' said Laird.

They shook hands and went their separate ways.

Laird was alone in the gallery a few days later when he looked up from his desk to see a familiar man walking towards him. Slugs of flesh poked between the overstrained buttons of his sweat-stained white shirt and his thighs rubbed together when he walked, making a swishing noise that made Laird think of two lumberjacks sawing through a log.

Uninvited, he sat down in the seat opposite Laird, wiped a film of sweat from his brow and placed his forearms on the desk. 'Can I help you?' said Laird, filling a plastic cup of water from the cooler behind him and taking a sip. He placed the cup on the desk between them.

'No,' said the man. 'But maybe *I* can help *you*.'

Laird leant back in his chair and crossed his arms.

The man raised his chin. 'I am Vinodh Vijaykumar,' he said. 'Boss of Badlu Santosh.'

'Badlu,' repeated Laird. 'Badlu. Ah, yes, of course.'

'You are an admirer, I believe, of his artistic abilities.'

'He has a gift,' said Laird. 'Given a chance, he could do very well for himself in a city like this.'

'Oh, and he would like to,' said Vinodh. 'Very much he would like to. But, you see, it's not that simple. Badlu is under contract. We possess his passport, his work permit. He cannot simply walk away from his job.'

'I see,' said Laird.

'I'd hate to see his, *Badlu's*, talent wasted, however' said Vinodh. 'My workers' – he clasped his hands together as if in prayer – 'are like sons to me.'

'Of course they are,' said Laird, icily.

'But *arrangements* can always be made,' said Vinodh, lowering his voice to a conspiratorial whisper and rubbing two fingers together in front of Laird's face.

'You want money?' said Laird, shifting in his seat. 'You want me to pay you to release Badlu from his contract with you, is that it?'

'A token amount to cover the paperwork, that is all,' said Vinodh. 'Let us say, fifty thousand dirhams? A trifling amount when you think what he could make for you in the long term.'

'That's a year's rent money,' laughed Laird. 'And even if I had it, I wouldn't give a fil to you.'

'Not a fil, eh?'

'That's right, Mr Vijaykumar. Now if you don't mind, I'm busy.'

The two men glared at each other until Vinodh stood up, sending his chair sliding backwards.

'So be it then,' said Vinodh, turning his back on Laird and heading for the door. 'Your so-called friend can break his back lifting bricks all day.'

From that day, the images ceased appearing on Laird's car and the next time he saw Badlu was several weeks later, curled up asleep around the back of the gallery amongst his colleagues. It distressed Laird to see that his hands were now callused and scratched, the gloves nowhere to be seen. His moustache, too, had lost its waxy sheen and shape, like a badly neglected privet hedge.

Standing over the slumbering Badlu, Laird retrieved a fifty dirham note from his wallet and was about to place it into the pocket of his overalls when Badlu's eyes flickered open. Seeing the money in Laird's hand, he gave a weak smile and pushed it away. Laird scrunched the note in his fist, embarrassed by his own condescension.

'I'm sorry, Badlu,' he said. 'I tried.'

Badlu waggled his head and slowly closed his eyes.

Vinodh Vijaykumar's body was found by his workers the following morning in the parking lot behind the gallery. A massive heart attack caused by the stress of the job, the police said – no foul play suspected. Laird watched from the back door of the gallery later that day as two police officers in a pick-up truck towed Vinodh's car away. As it passed, Laird saw the gorgon-like image etched into the dust of the car and it gave him goosebumps. He knew from his gap year that it was Kali, the Hindu goddess of destruction and wondered: could a picture literally scare a man to death? What if it had somehow come alive and... No, get a grip, Laird, he told himself, tugging the reigns of his imagination. Badlu had drawn the picture to jinx his boss, cast some portent of doom, that much was obvious, but to believe in magic was silly. And yet the path to Badlu's progression as an artist of some kind was now much clearer. There would be another boss, of course, but one, surely, who would be nowhere near as avaricious as the loathsome Vinodh Vijaykumar.

Laird waited patiently for Badlu to show his face but there was no sign of him. After several weeks he approached the labourers on the building site to enquire after his whereabouts, but Badlu, they told him, had absconded one night and hadn't been seen since. Smuggled himself back to India, perhaps, on one of the cargo *dhows* berthed along the Creek. Or, worse, flung himself into the rough waves that battered the corniche at Al Mamzar. Suicide or escape – these were, Laird was appalled to hear, such frequent occurrences among labourers that they barely warranted discussion in the camps where they lived.

It was the day after his visit to the camp that Laird's concern was laid to rest. He was walking to his car after locking up the gallery when there on the bonnet was another picture in the dust. An intricate and perfectly symmetrical butterfly freeing itself from a cocoon dangling from the branch of a palm tree. Laird looked around for signs of Badlu but there was nothing to be seen except for a set of deep footprints in the sand that began beside the car and disappeared at the edge of the road where a pair of battered old workboots, the soles worn wafer thin and the toes split open like a yawning purse, lay perishing under the blazing sun.

Whorelands

Me, Cooksy, Nips and Hopkins were on a mission to get laid. For five months we'd been dodging sniper fire and landmines, chasing ragheads out of Helmand Province. Not a woman in sight except on a computer screen, the couple of dykes serving in our unit and Cooksy's wank mags, which got passed around our base quicker than bird flu. So as soon as we arrived in Dubai for a few days R&R, we filled our wallets with condoms and cash and cut loose.

We started off in an Irish pub, got talking to a couple of expat girls from home who asked the questions we can never give honest answers to. Which regiment are you with? How long are you in town? Have you ever killed anyone? The usual shit.

We thought they might be up for it and we wouldn't need to hit the Palm Bay Hotel after all. Five drinks in and we hadn't made any inroads. But at least they laughed at our jokes, told us we were heroes doing Queen and country proud. Went all quiet when I told them I fucking hated being in the army – that I joined up because I'm from a dead end town with no jobs and how else was a lad with no qualifications going to see the world.

After a while, Hopkins, who has a way with words, got the prettiest one's number. Got a proper kiss too before the barman told them to quit it and remember which country they were in. Then Cooksy, bladdered by now, goes, 'Ever heard of the Trucial States, mate? This place was teepees and camels with sore arses before we came along,' and then we got told to sling our hooks and don't come back.

Hopkins and Nips decided to call it a night, while Cooksy and I, keen to accomplish our mission, headed to the Palm Bay, whose disco-bar on the top floor Sergeant Nugent refers to as 'a den of ill repute'. As if the dirty bastard hasn't checked it out himself. Any squaddie from Qatar to Kandahar knows the so-called 'Bay of Plenty'.

Africans, Eastern Europeans, Filipinos, Chinese, fat, thin, black, white... You name it, the Palm Bay stocks it in its seven-nights-a-week sex superstore. Eager girls, armed with fake fuck-me smiles and an invisible force field of perfume, line up to tell you in graphic detail why you should pick them, rather than one of the other 300 bints. We'd only been in the place five minutes when Cooksy, who has never been picky, threw in his lot with a chubby Oriental.

I went gallivanting and set my sights on this Beyoncé lookalike with beads in her hair. She was playing a quiz machine near the bar, sucking an alcopop through a curly straw. When she leaned over to put her drink down on a table next to the machine, I thought her arse cheeks would bust out of that tight white skirt like the Incredible Hulk's biceps. She clocked me looking at her and beckoned me over.

'Where are you from?' she said as I reached her side.

'England.'

'Good. I like English guys.' She picked up her drink, locked eyes on me as she sucked on the straw. She was trying to be all seductive but the serious pouting thing she had going on just made her look surly if no less fuckable.

'How much?'

'One thousand dirhams.'

'Three hundred.'

'It's three hundred just for a room here.'

'I don't want to stay here,' I said. 'Let's go to yours.'

'OK, but five hundred. I'm good, you'll see.'

'Alright,' I said. 'Five hundred. Let me say goodbye to my mate.'

*

She told the taxi driver to take us to a place called Whorelands. He nodded and pulled away into the street.

'What's funny?' she said when I started laughing.

'You've got to be fucking shitting me,' I said. 'Whorelands?'

'Yes. *Whorelands*, near Murraqabat,' she said, getting annoyed.

'If you say so,' I said, thinking her and the taxi driver were in cahoots.

After a few minutes silence she pointed to a big road sign we were passing.

It said: **HOR AL ANZ**.

'Ah, *that* whorelands,' I said, shaking my head, grinning. She didn't get the joke and I didn't have the heart to explain it.

Her place was a cramped studio apartment above an Egyptian restaurant in a downtrodden area that lived up to its name – or at least what it sounded like. The friend she shared it with was a thinner, paler-skinned version of her. She was curled up on the room's only bed watching a music channel on a tiny TV mounted on the wall. She'd been smoking a sheesha pipe – I could see the charcoal still smouldering away on the tinfoil. Orange flavour. Thank fuck for that sweet scent. I didn't want to smell all the sex that room had seen. Probably more than a porno movie-set or Russell Brand's tour bus. She said the friend would wait in the bathroom until we'd finished.

'Why can't she go out for a while?' I said.

'It's too late for her to be on the streets.'

'She's a prostitute,' I said. 'It's part of the job description isn't it?'

'She's not a prostitute. Works in the downstairs restaurant.'

'Right. So she's going to wait in there until we're finished?'

'It's no problem.'

'It's a fucking problem for *me*,' I said. 'Her listening to us.'

'Not listening. She will play music.'

She said something to the friend in their language and it stirred up a bit of debate that went on so long I started looking at my watch.

Eventually, sulking like Wayne Rooney after he's just been shown a red card, the friend snatched a portable radio from the bedside table and disappeared into the bathroom, slamming the door behind her. She switched on the radio and turned up the volume. I recognised the tune. It was 'Dance Wiv Me' by Calvin Harris featuring Dizzee Rascal. Nips always plays it to death back at base, says it reminds him of when he lost his virginity in the cloakroom of some skanky Northern nightclub.

We sat on the bed next to each other. Underneath the top sheets I could feel some kind of plastic cover. I appreciated this attempt at hygiene.

'What's your name?' I asked Beyoncé.

She said, 'Beyoncé.'

'Right, so I'm not the first person to think you look like her,' I said. 'Seriously, though, what's your real name?'

'Florence.'

'That's nice,' I said. 'Take off your clothes, Florence. I bet you've got a killer body under there.'

We sat on the bed undressing ourselves. I took a look around the gaff. It was no better or worse than our army base. Cramped and depressing. As far from a real home as a place could be outside of a prison cell. A plastic Jesus stared down at me from a wooden cross on the wall above the bed's headboard. There were dabs of red paint where the nails went in. I thought of the young boy we found hung from a goalpost on a football pitch outside a village near Kandahar last year. They had cut out his tongue, a half-burnt American flag stuffed into his bloody mouth.

'When was the last time you went home, Florence?' I asked, spotting a suitcase covered in dust lying on top of a wardrobe. We were both almost naked now. Her body was firm and golden brown and she had shaved between her legs.

She shook her head and wagged her finger in my face. I was getting too personal. I knew where she was coming from. There's stuff you have to keep a lid on sometimes just to keep going in life.

Without speaking we lay next to each other under the sheets for a while – I liked the feel of her warm, soft flesh pressed against the scars of my hard body – but when it came to fucking I couldn't do it. It was Jesus's fault. I'm no Bible basher but he looked so bloody holy up there, nailed to the cross. And there was I, preparing to bang a hooker on a spunk-stained bed. I'd done this kind of thing more times than I could remember, but not under the watchful eye of the son of God. It was a major turn off, truth be told. A potent stiffy-slayer.

Florence reached down and felt between my legs. I was embarrassed. You could barely call it a penis. Just a potential penis. She started tossing me off, but it was pointless – like trying to pump up a bicycle tyre with a hole in it.

'It's not okay?' she said, after a while.

'No,' I said. 'Not okay. Not really.'

'Something wrong?'

'Yeah. Why is Jesus above your bed?'

'He protects me from harm.'

'Well, I can't do it,' I said. 'Not while he's looking. Can't you take him down?'

'Where shall I put him?'

'Fucking cutlery draw. I don't know.'

She looked upset. There was a long silence as she thought about it, wondering whether I'd still cough up the money if Jesus stayed put. We both realised it was no simple task. He seemed to be superglued to the wall. Then the music in the bathroom stopped and the room was silent again.

'Hey, are you listening in there?' I said.

'Sorry, battery finished,' the friend said.

She filled the silence by flushing the toilet. Then she started running all the taps. Then the shower. Which made me feel like taking a piss.

'Listen,' I said to Florence. 'Can I get some sleep? Just a couple of hours?'

'My friend must sleep too,' Florence said.

'Well, there's room for three of us if we squeeze together,' I said.

'OK,' Florence said. 'Same money?'

'Same money,' I said.

She called her friend out of the bathroom.

'I *wasn't* listening,' the friend said, glowering at me.

I took a piss, then we all climbed into the bed together and switched off the light. I must have fallen asleep in seconds.

When I awoke a few hours later it was just Florence and I in the bed. She slept curled up, her knees raised and her fists clenched under her chin like a little kid. I put on my jeans and went over to the curtains at the end of the room and pulled them open. There were sliding doors behind them that opened on to a small balcony so I went outside and smoked a cigarette. It was just beginning to get light and a few shops were already open on the street below. A bald Arab man in a tracksuit appeared on the next balcony along and stared at me.

'These *sharmoutas*,' he said, shaking his head.

I didn't understand and the look I gave him must have said as much.

'Prostitutes,' he said. 'This used to be a respectable building.' And then he went back into his apartment.

Florence joined me after a few minutes. She was wearing some kind of colourful, shapeless tunic and drinking water from a cracked pint glass.

'I fucking hate my job, Florence,' I said. 'I don't want to go back.' I heard my voice starting to break so I shut myself up. It was true, though. Each time I flew back to Afghanistan I wondered whether my time was almost up, whether there was a Taliban bullet with my name on it.

Florence sipped her water and nodded. 'I also wish for another life.'

We stood silent for a while and watched a bunch of bearded Pakistani men load heavy furniture from a truck into a shop. A man rode past with clean laundry piled impossibly high on the back of his bicycle. He struggled to keep his balance as he weaved in and out of the traffic, which seemed hell-bent on not letting him through. I bet they all hated their jobs.

'What's stopping you from doing something else?' I asked Florence.

'Madam has my passport. I have to pay off my debt to her, then maybe I will get a job in a clothes shop in a mall. Zara or GAP.'

'Have you got family to support back home then?' It was usually the case with these girls.

'My family is dead,' Florence said. 'Only my brother in Addis Ababa. He has his own family now'

'I'm an orphan, too,' I said, which was sort of true. My mother topped herself when I was nine and my father hasn't given a flying a fuck about me since he shacked up with his new woman and had another kid. 'We're all alone in the world, eh, Florence?'

She turned away from me and leaned over the rail of the balcony, looking down onto the street. I took her hand and squeezed it but there was no response.

'This is true about your parents?' she said, giving me a searching look.

'I wouldn't lie about something like that,' I said.

After a moment she gave my hand a squeeze back. I told her I'd like to see her again the next time I was in Dubai, so long as the Taliban didn't shoot me first. She laughed at this and said she would pray for me every night. I said maybe we could go and see a movie together. She said I shouldn't say that if I didn't mean it. She would get upset if I went back on my word. So we swapped mobile numbers and email addresses and then went back inside and got fully dressed.

On the way out I looked at Jesus and gave him a wink.

Florence caught me doing it and burst out laughing. She had a beautiful smile and the noise that came out made her sound younger than she looked.

'Good,' she said, clasping her hands together. 'Now Jesus will protect you too.'

I didn't believe that for a second but I did believe I'd see Florence again. That was good enough.

The Orange Tie

It was Friday evening and Aaron was in the kitchen preparing dinner and listening to Dieter singing in the shower when the doorbell rang. The noise rattled him. Few people visited their villa in Mirdif, a dull suburb on the margins of the city.

He opened the door to find Juma, his Emirati neighbour and his eldest son, Mohammed – a scrawny twenty-one-year-old with a downy moustache and eyebrows that fused untidily on the bridge of his nose.

Juma's girth tested the seams of a cotton *kandora* the flawless white of cosmetically-enhanced teeth – Aaron had never seen him wear anything else – while Mohammed wore an ill-fitting navy suit and powder blue shirt. He held in his right hand an orange necktie.

'Mr Juma, hi!' said Aaron, stricken by self-consciousness. He wore only a pair of faded red football shorts, a band of white skin visible between the top of the shorts and his suntanned torso.

'Sorry… give me a minute?' said Aaron. 'I was just in the middle of something.'

Leaving the front door ajar he went through the hallway and into the kitchen to take a saucepan of water off the boil. Then he went back into the hallway and into his bedroom where he scrambled into the first things that came to hand: one of Dieter's stripy work shirts and a pair of bobbling tracksuit bottoms.

Passing the villa's empty second bedroom on the way back, he shut its door, making sure he heard the click of the latch.

Seeing that the front door had now swung wide open – Juma and Mohammed peering in – Aaron realised with dismay that there was no way of letting Dieter know they had visitors. Sensing that whatever they wanted wasn't so trivial that it could be discussed on the doorstep, Aaron ushered the two men through the hallway and into the kitchen. He motioned for them to take a seat at the dining table.

In the three months they had lived at the villa, Aaron and Dieter's dealings with Juma had been limited to a handful of brief and stilted conversations in the street outside their homes. As for Mohammed, Aaron noticed only that he was painfully shy and drove his red Audi TT convertible with a cautiousness that, for a young male Emirati, bordered on the unpatriotic. Their presence in the villa unsettled Aaron, and yet at the same time he was strangely honoured. He thought back to when he first came to Dubai and had associated all Emiratis with wealth and prestige. It was the *kandora* that did it. Those immaculate white robes conferred on their male wearer an air of august nobility.

Feeling a film of sweat break out on his forehead, Aaron opened the window, allowing a light breeze to find its way in.

'Would you like some coffee?' asked Aaron.

'Please,' said Juma. 'No milk.'

'Mohammed?' Aaron held up the cafetiere.

'The same, please.'

'Your family is well, Mr Juma?' asked Aaron, acutely aware that etiquette in this part of the world demanded that the start of every conversation be restricted to mutual enquiries after the health of close relations. He was conscious, also, of the fact that whenever he talked to Arabs he tended to emulate their way of speaking, that chary way they had of phrasing questions as statements.

'*Il humdilillah* they are very good,' said Juma. 'And yours, in the UK?'

'Very well, thank you.'

'You have been sunbathing?' Juma was referring to two towels and a pair of damp swimming trunks that were piled on top of the washing machine.

'Yes, at Al Mamzar,' said Aaron. 'We've got to be so careful in this part of the world, though.' He checked himself. 'About the sun, I mean.'

'Yes, it is never sunny in England,' said Juma, a note of triumph in his voice. Aaron recalled Juma once mentioning he had been a student in Manchester in the early eighties. For some reason he had only lasted a single semester before returning to Dubai. Aaron found it impossible to imagine Juma wandering the streets of that northern English city, clad in trousers, boots and a thick coat to bar the cold bite of autumn.

Pouring the coffee, Aaron noticed that Mohammed was feeding the orange necktie through his fingers as if it were a string of prayer beads. The laces were undone on his shoes, tongues slipping sideways exposing white sports socks. He emanated a pungent aroma of newness, as if everything he wore had just been unwrapped.

Aaron handed the men two mugs of coffee and they sipped cautiously. They had chosen to sit next to each other, leaving Aaron no choice but to sit opposite them, as though under interrogation.

From the bathroom came the muffled sound of water spattering the plastic base of the shower. Aaron silently prayed that a naked, soap-lathered Dieter wouldn't burst into the kitchen, as he was wont to do, demanding to know where the fuck the clean towels were.

Juma cleared his throat and touched his hand to his chest. He placed his mug on the table and slowly, carefully turned it so that the handle pointed... where, exactly? Mecca, perhaps, thought Aaron. It was, after all, Friday, the Holiest day of the week for Muslims.

'Mr Aaron,' said Juma at last, 'Mohammed's employer would like him to spend time at their London office where he will be required to wear Western clothing. However the problem is...' Tugging the tie from Mohammed's grasp, Juma held it aloft, pinching the thin end between thumb and forefinger, as if holding a dead, venomous snake. '*This* is giving Mohammed big headache,' he said. 'We try and try but we cannot make into a knot. So I say we must consult Mr Aaron, an Englishman. *Inshallah* he will know how.'

Aaron felt his body relax. 'You've certainly come to the

right man,' he said, smiling at Mohammed. 'Clothes maketh the man, Mr Juma, and I'm very particular about the way I knot my tie.'

'So you will help him?' asked Juma.

'It would be an honour,' said Aaron. 'Shall we go into the garden? It's cooler out there... and our air conditioning isn't the best.' He was thinking about Dieter, still in the shower, oblivious to the visitors.

Juma swallowed the last of his coffee in one gulp and stood up. He made a dismissive gesture toward the tie that now lay coiled on the table. 'Thank you,' he said. 'But I am not a fan of such... accessories.'

When Juma had gone, Aaron fetched one of his own ties from the bedroom, then returned to the kitchen. Through the open window he could see Mohammed in the garden. He was sitting beside the swimming pool on one of several white plastic chairs, his shirt collar turned up ready.

It took Aaron several minutes to teach Mohammed a basic Windsor knot. Aaron suggested he might want to learn a bow-tie too, in case he was ever invited to more formal events. But Mohammed, standing up and glancing at his watch, apologised and said he had to be elsewhere.

'Some other time, perhaps,' said Aaron, doubting whether Mohammed would ever return.

As soon as Mohammed had left, Aaron went into the bathroom to tell Dieter what had happened. At the back of his mind was the slightly embarrassing thought that this was by far the most exciting thing that had happened to them since moving to Mirdif.

'Befriending the natives, huh?' said Dieter. He was standing in front of the mirror above the sink, trimming his sideburns into thin points with electric clippers. He was wearing a white towelling dressing gown that Aaron had stolen from the hotel on their first holiday together. 'Just be careful. People like them don't like people like us, remember?'

Exactly two weeks later, Mohammed returned alone. He wore a *kandora* and carried an expensive-looking leather-bound notebook filled with English words whose pronunciation baffled him and an internet printout of the London Underground.

'I'm a little surprised,' said Aaron when they were in the kitchen. 'I wasn't really sure I'd see you again.'

He rifled through the cupboards, trying to find the strong Turkish coffee he had bought from the spice *soukh* in Naif the previous week. Dieter was in the garden fishing dead leaves out of the swimming pool with a net, an unlit Marlborough Light dangling from his mouth.

'I have many questions for you,' said Mohammed. 'Maybe you will get fed up with me.'

'You couldn't have come at a better time,' said Aaron. 'Dieter's been pestering me all day to watch some arty black and white film.' He glanced out the window, lowered his voice. 'All I really want to see is James Bond save the world.'

They sat next to each other at the kitchen table. Mohammed smelt strongly of both incense and CK One, as if he was wearing one of his father's *kandoras* and was trying to eclipse Juma's traditional oud-based scent with his own modern aroma.

'What have you got here then?' asked Aaron, taking the leather notebook from Mohammed and randomly opening it to a page headed **CURSE WORDS**.

Aaron could make out the words 'Bastard' and 'Wanker' and, presumably, their Arabic translations beside them.

Mohammed grinned mischievously and Aaron saw for the first time that he had good teeth, straight and even as a picket fence.

He was secretly pleased by the unexpected icebreaker, worried that Mohammed would turn out to be surly or pious. 'Well, well,' said Aaron, reciprocating his pupil's toothy grin. 'Your English is more advanced than I thought.'

From that day onwards, Mohammed turned up without fail at six o'clock every Friday evening. There were three months before he started his new job and he was eager to practise his English, learn all he could about London – where to eat, live, shop. For these meetings he invariably wore his *kandora,* the *ghuttra* worn tied up around his head, turban-style, the way Aaron had seen other Emirati youths wear them in the shopping malls, along with the obligatory designer sunglasses.

Aaron told Mohammed about the Arabic restaurants and *sheesha* cafes on the Edgware Road, urged him to visit them whenever he felt homesick. He told him about Selfridges and Harvey Nichols and the best clothing shops on Bond Street. Dieter, warming to Mohammed after an initial period of aloofness, teased him about being a Chelsea football fan when surely he should support their rivals Arsenal, whose team shirts bore the corporate logo of Emirates Airlines. With each visit, Mohammed became more talkative, shedding layers of adolescent diffidence that laid bare an easy-going charm.

When one week Mohammed presented them with a large plate of *baklawa* and *sambusas* as a token of his gratitude, they were genuinely moved.

'My mother made them,' said Mohammed. 'Special recipe.'

Aaron wondered which of Juma's three pretty wives he should thank next time he saw them in the street.

Mohammed's visits usually lasted around an hour and Dieter and Aaron were, if not quite glad of the company, grateful for the way they broke up the tedium of their weekends. The visits allowed them, too, a glimpse of Emirati life, an enigma to Western expats. They didn't know anybody who was on more than nodding terms with a local. Dieter said it was a rare opportunity that they should take advantage of.

'I'm going to ask Mohammed about the sleeping arrangements between Juma and his wives,' he told Aaron one evening. They were at a newly-opened Chinese restaurant in the Downtown area of the city. Oriental music that could barely be heard above the murmur of diners played from an indiscernible source.

'You are joking,' said Aaron.

'I mean do they have a rota system or what?' asked Dieter.

'Something like that, probably.'

Dieter raised an eyebrow. 'Maybe the horny old devil has them all at the same time.'

'Keep your voice down.'

77

'I don't see any locals here.'

Aaron looked around the restaurant then pointed at Dieter with a chopstick.

'Don't you dare ask Mohammed about that.'

'He wouldn't mind,' said Dieter. 'We know him well enough now.'

'It's not about whether he *minds*,' said Aaron, frowning. 'It's just plain rude. I'm serious, Dieter, you simply don't ask an Emirati that kind of question. End of story.'

'Hey, *okay*… Message understood.'

Mohammed's weekly presence, though not unwelcome, put them on tenterhooks. Tactile affection was strictly prohibited and they were careful to ensure he never wandered around the villa unattended to discover that it contained only one double bed. Dieter, who had a chronic fear of being incarcerated in a foreign prison, even went as far as removing from the shelf in the lounge a framed photo of the pair of them at the Sydney Mardi Gras, on account of the drag queen lurking in the background. In its place he put a picture downloaded from the internet of an anonymous young blonde woman riding a carousel at a funfair.

'Oh, come on!' said Aaron when he saw it for the first time. 'Isn't that a little excessive?'

'Don't you think he finds it strange?' said Dieter. 'That neither of us have a girlfriend or wife.'

'Do it if it makes you feel better but that girl is kind of stunning.'

'You're point being?'

'Cute as you are, you're no Brad Pitt.'

'Fine, I'll downgrade,' said Dieter, but the picture stayed. A reminder, if nothing else, of the need for extra vigilance.

One day, when Aaron interrupted their tutorial to take a phone call in another room, Mohammed wandered into the lounge where Dieter was lying smoking in front of the TV.

'Hello Mohammed,' said Dieter. He lowered the volume of the film with the remote and stubbed out his cigarette. 'How are your lessons coming along?'

'This is a friend?' asked Mohammed, pointing at the photograph of the blonde woman.

'No, that's Petra... my wife.'

Mohammed walked over to the photograph and picked it up. He held it as though it were a rare and ancient book written in a language he didn't understand. 'She is very beautiful,' he said. 'She doesn't want to live in Dubai?'

'In a year or two, perhaps,' said Dieter. 'Her mother is sick. For now, it's better she stays in Germany to look after her.'

Mohammed studied the photograph for several more seconds before carefully replacing it on the shelf.

Early one Friday afternoon, Aaron and Dieter were lying on sun loungers in the garden. They had just moved from beside the swimming pool and into the shade of the tall garden wall that was a little higher than the roof of the villa. The sun had had the sky to itself all day but it was about to be ambushed by an armada of thick white clouds drifting in from the east.

They had been grocery shopping that morning and were

drinking freshly-made margaritas and picking from a plate of sliced mango that sat on the tiled floor between them.

Realising that Dieter had eaten the last slice of mango, Aaron cleared his throat with theatrical emphasis.

'I'll get you some more in a minute,' said Dieter. 'There's more in the fruit bowl.'

Aaron stood up and brushed his bare foot gently against the side of Dieter's face. Dieter responded by gripping Aaron's ankle and pulling him towards him. Aaron lost his balance and collapsed on top of Dieter. He manoeuvred himself so that their faces were inches apart. They kissed, Dieter caressing the nape of Aaron's neck and burying his fingers into the hair on the back of his head. Dieter's fingers were sticky from the mango and the way they stuck to his hair made Aaron laugh through his nose and pull away.

'What's wrong?' asked Dieter.

Aaron was about to answer when a noise came from the kitchen, a piece of cutlery clattering into the sink. Dieter was the first to respond, springing to his feet as though he had just sat on a nailbrush.

They looked across at the kitchen window to see Mohammed's startled face staring at them through the glass. He turned and fled. They heard the front door slam shut.

Aaron buried his head in his hands.

When he looked up he saw that Dieter was staring at the top of the garden wall as though Juma and a posse of homo-hating Islamic fundamentalists were about to leap over it, curved *khanjar* daggers clasped, pirate-like, between their bared teeth.

'Didn't you close the front door properly?' said Aaron.

'Hey! Take it easy, I was carrying all the shopping bags remember,' said Dieter. He picked up his margarita, downed the last drop. 'You think he'll say anything?'

'How should I know!' said Aaron. Going into the villa, he made a point of shutting the door firmly behind him. 'See, not exactly difficult, is it?' he muttered, loudly enough for Dieter to hear.

Mohammed didn't come back that evening or any other evening. On the one occasion he passed the two men in the street he looked hurriedly away.

Two weeks later, on a cool, grey morning, Aaron and Dieter watched from the window of the spare room as Juma and their Sri Lankan houseboy loaded two large Samsonite suitcases into the trunk of a Land Rover. Mohammed appeared soon after, dressed in jeans and a T-shirt, and got into the car before it disappeared down the street.

'If he's told his father...' said Dieter.

'I suppose we'll soon find out, won't we?'

The following evening they were sitting on the sofa in the lounge, watching television, when Dieter said, 'I think we should leave Mirdif.'

Aaron tossed a handful of pistachio nuts into his mouth instead of replying. He continued to stare at the TV.

'Rudy Van Beek's got a spare room in his villa,' continued Dieter. 'Two minutes walk from the beach and the rent is cheap.'

'You want to go back to Jumeirah?'

'We stick out like a sore thumb here. It's all families and couples.'

Aaron turned to face Dieter. He pressed his back against the arm of the sofa, a chasm opening up between them. 'So what are we?'

'You know what I mean,' said Dieter. 'In England you would call this suburbia, yes? A place where people go to spawn. Or retire and die.'

'You're thirty-five next month, Dieter,' said Aaron, a touch of exasperation in his voice. 'There comes a point where it all becomes undignified.'

'What does?'

'Clubbing. After-hours parties at some rich dickhead's mansion, hanging out with twenty-one-year-old models. It's fucking cheesy, and we agreed, Dieter. We agreed to leave all that shit behind. Remember?'

'I never thought moving out here was going to be...' Dieter forced the words out. 'So *boring*. We don't do anything, don't go anywhere, and nobody will come to us because Mirdif is... well, we might as well be in the middle of the fucking Sahara with all the traffic you have to battle through. Anyway, after what happened... I just feel really uncomfortable.'

'So we just up sticks every time we get a bit paranoid? Can't we at least think about this?'

'My mind's made up, Aaron,' said Dieter. 'I'm moving back to Jumeirah next month. If you've got any sense, so will you.'

Aaron remained in Mirdif for several weeks after Dieter moved out, expecting him to change his mind. They stayed in touch by phone only to quibble over possessions and utility bills. When Aaron realised that Dieter wasn't coming back and that he could no longer afford to pay the rent alone he moved into a studio apartment in Al Barsha with a balcony the size of a pulpit and a bathroom that smelled of damp. Gradually their calls petered out and Aaron immersed himself in his job at a publishing company. He took up yoga with a female friend, read self-help books and implored friends from home to come and visit. Every Friday night his thoughts still drifted to Dieter, undoubtedly partying the night away in some private mansion with the city's gay glitterati.

Three months later Aaron heard through friends that Dieter's advertising agency had transferred him to Singapore where they were launching a new branch. When Aaron received a grovelling email from Dieter saying he would be returning to Dubai in a year when they could perhaps try again, make a fresh start, Aaron didn't reply. Nor could he bring himself to delete the email.

Early one weekday evening, almost a year after leaving Mirdif, Aaron was sitting in a corner of his local Starbucks reading a newspaper when he noticed Mohammed sitting at a table on the opposite side of the room. He was with four young Emirati men, all of whom wore traditional dress. Two of them, Mohammed included, had substituted their *ghuttra* for brightly-coloured baseball caps. They were having a friendly argument, raising their voices, mock-punching each other and laughing.

He watched the group for a short while, wondering whether he should finish his coffee and leave, when

Mohammed suddenly got up and walked over to the condiment stand. Aaron found himself raising his hand to get his attention, half-expecting a negative, perhaps even hostile, response, but to his relief Mohammed smiled and walked over to him. Aaron saw that Mohammed's skinny frame had filled out with muscle, his shoulders broader. He had shaved off his moustache.

'Mister Aaron?'

Aaron stood up, waited for Mohammed to offer his hand, but saw that it held a sheaf of napkins and sachets of sugar.

'My father told me you moved away,' said Mohammed.

'Almost a year ago,' said Aaron. 'I live in Al Barsha now.'

Mohammed's eyes rested briefly on Aaron's chest. Aaron looked down expecting to see a stain or an undone button but found nothing amiss. They sat down opposite each other at the small round table and Mohammed pocketed the napkins and sachets.

'You're no longer in London?' said Aaron.

'I am,' said Mohammed. 'This is a holiday. I fly back to England tomorrow.'

'The big city is treating you well?'

'I love it.' Glancing about the room, Mohammed lowered his voice. 'I have a British girlfriend, Serena. She is extremely beautiful. Actually she looks a lot like Petra.'

'Sorry, Petra?' Aaron was baffled.

'You know! Dieter's wife, the woman in the...'

Aaron remembered the picture. 'She was just a stranger,' he said, allowing himself a weak laugh. 'Dieter seemed to think he needed to, well…' He trailed off, took a sip of coffee he knew would be tepid by now.

Two small starbursts of pink coloured Mohammed's cheeks. He adjusted his baseball cap needlessly. 'I get it,' he said.

Mohammed swept some stray sugar grains off the surface of the table with the side of his hand and leaned in toward Aaron. 'In London,' he said, 'my girlfriend likes to show me cool places. Soho, Camden, Notting Hill. You find all kinds of people there. People that my father would….' He smiled, shaking his head. 'He is of a generation that remembers the Dubai of camels and no air conditioning. Sometimes I think the world moves too quickly for him, you understand?'

Aaron wasn't sure that he did but he nodded anyway.

'So, your father…' Aaron, paused, wondering whether he was about to overstep the mark. 'He doesn't mind you having a non-Muslim girlfriend?'

'There are many things I don't tell my father,' said Mohammed, smiling. He paused, waiting for the smile to disappear before adding softly, 'Many things.'

A long silence fell between them and Aaron felt a sadness seeping into him. He felt sad for assuming that Mohammed, whom he had got to know so well, and who had shone with such sensitivity and intelligence, would inform his father what he had seen that day. This assumption had instigated the end of his and Dieter's relationship, by far the longest and, on reflection, happiest he had ever had. For a moment he felt like he was going to shed tears and fought them back, trying to push Dieter from his thoughts. Depressed and alone in

Mirdif during the weeks after Dieter had left him, he had done all his crying. Recently he had thought about handing in his resignation and heading home to England. Only the possibility of he and Dieter making a fresh start on his eventual return to Dubai made him stay. He decided, now, that he would reply to Dieter's email as soon as he reached home. He hoped it wasn't too late.

'How is Mr Dieter?' said Mohammed, as if reading his thoughts.

'He's fine. Dieter's fine.'

'Good. Please tell him I was asking after him.'

Mohammed's friends were getting up to leave. One of them was clapping his hands and calling over to him. '*Yalla, habibi*!'

Mohammed ignored him. 'Look me up in London,' he said. 'My company is in West Kensington. I gave you the name before, remember?'

'I remember it,' said Aaron.

Again Aaron caught Mohammed looking at his chest.

'It suits you,' said Mohammed.

Aaron looked down again. He realised he was wearing the orange tie. A couple of weeks into their acquaintance Mohammed had insisted he have it, claiming the colour didn't match any of his shirts. This was only the third time Aaron had ever worn it.

When he looked up, Mohammed offered him his hand. Aaron shook it. Then he watched Mohammed walk out of the cafe and join his friends in the street.

Suzie Kaminski versus the Most Evil Man in the World

Some years ago, when I was working as an air hostess based in Abu Dhabi, I met the most evil man in the world. I was dating Corsten at the time, a handsome lawyer with springy hair and a Mustang convertible. Corsten was the one who suggested I get the implants. He knew how I felt about my breasts, what little there was of them, but if I hated being flat-chested then I hated even more the idea of being sliced open, poked into, stitched up like a goddamn baseball. Corsten kept telling me it would boost my confidence. Think of all those tight tops and bikinis you've bought but never worn, Suzie, he said. Think of a life without padded bras. In the end I gave in. Not for myself, you understand, but because I was real keen on Corsten and got it into my crazy, loved-up little mind that if I stayed as I was I might lose him to some floozy with a cleavage the size of the Grand Canyon. Pathetic I know.

I asked Fatima, an Arabic work friend of mine, who had recently gone from a B to a D cup herself, to recommend a surgeon. Fatima was fed up with working for a low budget airline and was desperate for a job with one of the big glamour companies like Emirates, who employed the best-looking girls. She showed me her half-grapefruits one day in the toilets at Heathrow. I touched them. They were pretty neat. Firm and perky with hardly any scars at all. She said they were the work of a Swiss surgeon at some fancy place over in Dubai. It was a female-only clinic in a quiet part of Umm Suqeim and it specialised in breast augmentation, rhinoplasty and endoscopic brow lifts. When I was next in the area I booked an appointment and went for a consultation. Within a month I was on the operating table, and Silicon Valley had a whole new meaning to me.

Anyway, when I came round after the operation I felt real groggy, which the surgeon said was natural and all, but he thought I'd better stay the night as a precautionary measure. I didn't mind. I had a TV in my room and the latest Barbara Kingsolver paperback to pass the time away. I wasn't due back at work for a few days so I told myself to relax. A few weeks and I'd be playing volleyball on the beach in a bikini, boobs bouncing around like a *Baywatch* babe.

It was around 9 p.m. when a sour-faced female nurse came around with a glass of water and two little capsules. She made me swallow them in front of her, then turned off the TV and lights. Before she went she said that if I needed anything I should press the buzzer beside my bed. Press it and wait for me, she said, even if it is just to go to the bathroom. I was still pretty pissed about not having an en suite for the money I was paying and told her that if she would just tell me where it was I could go alone. I wasn't some frail old coot who needed my goddamn butt wiped. She ignored me and was insistent – like, *real* insistent – that I call her if I needed anything, anything at all. As she left the room she gave me this stern look. I felt like a kid who's just been told to keep her hands out of the cookie jar.

Around 4 a.m. I woke up busting for a pee. I was about to press the buzzer to call the nurse but I couldn't see the worth in it. I was clear-headed, could walk about just fine, and since the clinic was only a small two storey building I guessed the bathroom wouldn't be far away.

I got out of bed wearing only my jogging pants, and put on my slippers and bath robe. I tried to tie the belt of the robe but the towelling material chafed my sore nipples real bad so I left it open. I walked out of my room and closed the door quietly behind me. I found the john in seconds and relieved my grateful bladder.

On the way back I realised that I didn't know which room was mine. The doors to all the rooms were painted the same pale blue and weren't numbered. Eventually I narrowed the choice down to two doors near the end of the corridor and chose the one on my left. I opened it.

It was real dark so I had to stick my head right in to see anything. When my eyes adjusted to the darkness I saw a man in a loose-fitting tunic and white skull-cap sitting on a chair beside a single bed. He was sleeping with his chin on his chest, a little tilt of the head accompanying every intake of breath. He was framed by a large curtained window behind him. Two moths danced across the dark green fabric of the curtains.

Asleep on the bed, lying face-up under a crisp white sheet, was a skinny bearded guy whose large feet stuck out at the end of the mattress. Such gross feet! Pus-yellow calluses thick as bison hide, a thickness built up, I guess, from trekking across some jagged hell of a place. Made me wanna get my pedicure kit and go to town on those piggies. Something drew me toward the bed, and as I walked over to it, my slippers real quiet on the linoleum floor, I saw that the man sitting on the chair was holding a pistol in his lap. Looked just like the Berreta M9 my Uncle Zed used to shoot racoons with from the veranda when we lived up in Mariposa County. I guess I should have got the hell out of there after seeing that thing, but I was real curious about the man in the bed. To have an armed bodyguard, I knew that he must be real famous or important.

Standing beside the bed, I saw that the man's beard was long, straggly and grey-black, a hash-sign of bandages criss-crossing his thin nose. There was a patch of shaved, raw-looking skin on his chin where he seemed to have had work done. Some sort of implant I guess. I was thinking he must have been as ugly as a moose to want to change the way he looked so bad. I kinda felt sorry for the poor guy. I stood right over him, trying to get a closer look at his face.

And then he opened his eyes.

I heard this pathetic little whimpering noise, realised it came from me. I wanted to flee that room like a mouse from a viper pit, but felt like I was in the grip of a giant fist, my body stiff with fright. Those eyes I'd seen before. Hell, who hadn't! Images flashed in my mind like fragments of a terrible nightmare. The faces of innocents smeared in blood. Limbless bodies pulled from rubble. The president choking back tears in his speech to the nation. If I hadn't known of his terrible past I might have said his eyes were soulful, but they held a strange power that cloaked me in dread. I sure was glad I'd just taken a leak.

He stared at me for what seemed like minutes, and then his eyes lowered a little and fixed on an area below my collarbone. Looking down, I realised that my bath robe was wide open, my bruised and scarred breasts fully exposed. I caught a little movement on his lips, a slightly protruding tongue – appreciation, lust? Hell, I don't know. I guess one of the drawbacks to being on the run from the FBI all those years is that you don't get laid all that much. He sure liked what he saw, though, couldn't tear those peepers away.

Anyway, I could hardly believe what he did next. Only propped himself up on his elbows, then shot out his right arm, as if to offer me a friendly handshake. No way, misterman! I thought. I ain't no Republican but I'm firmly with politicians of the ass-kicking kind when it comes to dealing with these Al Qaeda fucks. Goddamn assholes ruined the lives of thousands of good, hard-working American citizens so stick your olive branch up your filthy, hell-bound butt! But what he actually did was grab one of my breasts, squeeze it with his cold, bony hand. I slapped it away like it was some darned mosquito, then wrapped my robe as tightly as I could around me.

'Lousy pervert!' I whispered. He may not have understood English but he sure as shit knew from my tone of voice that I was in no mood for seduction. 'Goddamn filthy turd-eating hog-fucker!'

A raging hurricane of fury had replaced the fear in me, and even his bodyguard sitting there with that Beretta didn't scare me none. Uncle Zed would've sure been proud.

Then this crazy idea took shape in my mind, planted itself there and refused to budge. It wouldn't be revenge, as such. I'd need the electric chair and a whole bunch of medieval torture tools for *that* shit, but I was gonna do my bit for the Free World if it was the last thing I did. The face of evil was staring me, Suzie Kaminski, right in the goddamn face and hear this: there's no folk that knows me good who'll say I'm the surrendering type of girl. No, sir.

'Just you wait, mister,' I said, 'Just you wait right there.' And then I ran from the room and began to scream at the top of my voice and bang on all the doors in the corridor. 'Intruder! Wake up, wake up, there are men in the clinic!' I hollered, loud as I could. 'Creeping around as we sleep. Intruders, spying on our half-naked bodies. Shame on them! Shame!'

I knew there was a chance that the other patients might think I had had a bad reaction to my medication, that they might tell me to shut up and go back to sleep you crazy American bitch. But within seconds they began to emerge from their rooms, semi-conscious and stumbling like zombies, bandaged and bruised, their faces laced with stitches. My plan, if you could call it that, relied on most of the other patients being Muslims, and therefore most likely to be pissed by the idea of a male stranger prowling amongst them, and so it proved. One Arab woman, who was lean and tall and had one of those hooked noses that reminded me of an eagle, had a walking stick and waved it around like she was a *real* hellcat. 'Where, sister?' she asked, taking me by my arm. 'Where is the beast? *Inshallah* we will beat him till he bleeds.' With this fierce warrior, this Arabian Boudicca beside me, I felt, like, *totally* invincible.

By now about a dozen of us had congregated in the corridor, all in various states of undress and bodily disrepair, and there I was, little Suzie Kaminski, barely a hundred and twenty pounds and too short to be a cheerleader, leading the attack in my tatty old *Sesame Street* slippers and pink bathrobe.

When we burst into the room I noticed a chill in the air that wasn't there before. The window was wide open, curtains swaying. We heard a car engine being turned on outside. Several of us ran to the window and pulled the curtains apart. The two men were down in the car park, the big bodyguard lifting his bag-a-bones boss into the back seat of a Toyota Land Cruiser with blacked out windows. They drove off, the wheels screeching and skidding across the parking lot. A light breeze carried the whiff of burning rubber up to us as we stood gathered at the window. The women flung foul-mouthed abuse into the night air, shook their fists and glowered like raging gargoyles. Some of the abuse was in Arabic, which sounded doubly furious. They sure have some weird and wonderful insults, the Arabs. Things like, 'uncircumcised son of a camel-loving bald whore' and, 'he who licks the sole of Satan's sandal.' Some folks think they're real chaste, those women of the Gulf, but I guess they've inherited a kick-ass streak from their Bedouin ancestors which makes them tougher than a quarterback on steroids. A couple of them were doing a victory jig, whooping and clapping, as though they had just castrated a serial rapist and there was a million bucks reward for his dismembered dick. All that elation was real infectious and I found myself joining in, the aches and pains of the operation numbed by the adrenalin coursing through me.

Eventually two nurses came and herded us back to our rooms. They looked real shocked by all the hullabaloo and were shooting each other worried glances, but they didn't say anything. I felt real tired at the end of all that and fell into a deep and satisfying sleep.

In the morning a doctor came and discharged me. There was no mention at all of the events of the previous night. I began to think that maybe it had been a weird dream induced by those little pills. When Corsten came to pick me up, however, he parked close to where the getaway car had sped off and as we drove away I saw skid marks on the parking lot. I knew then that that shit was real, every second of it.

We were driving down Sheikh Zayed Road toward Abu Dhabi, passing Ibn Battuta Mall, when Corsten pushed his sunglasses to the back of his head and I noticed that he was starting to recede a little at the sides. I thought about me being only twenty-two and having a bald boyfriend. It didn't bother me, just like my small breasts shouldn't have bothered him. 'Hey,' I said, ruffling his hair. 'Maybe you should think about getting a weave.'

He pushed my hand away and ignored me. He looked a little pissed. After a few minutes he said, 'So... how'd the op go?'

'Fine,' I said.

'You won't regret it,' he said. 'I'll be the envy of every guy.'

When he dropped me off at my apartment I told him that maybe he shouldn't come in because the medication had given me a migraine and I needed to sleep. I said I'd call him in a day or two. Maybe three.

He looked down at my chest with a leer. 'So, uh, how long before Corsten gets to stroke the new puppies?' He was practically drooling.

'Real soon, baby,' I said, 'Real soon.'

I had an urge just then to tell him that, actually, he had been beaten to it but I stopped myself. Corsten never did lay a finger on those puppies, though, and six months later I got the damn things taken out.

The Fidelity of
Abbas Ali Khan

Abbas Ali Khan glances at the clock on the dashboard.
It is almost 2 a.m. and in less than fifteen minutes he
will be watching the cricket at the Rainbow Cafe in
Satwa. This is to be his final fare of the night. Slowing
down as he approaches the destination, his fingers drum
out a cheery syncopation on the rim of the steering
wheel.

'We are here, Madam,' he says. 'Rolla Street?'

Concerned by the lack of response, he pulls up to the
kerb and twists round to look into the back of the cab.

His passenger has fallen asleep. She lays on her side
facing the front of the car, her bent knees breaching the
gap between the seats. Though she lays perfectly still,
Abbas can detect the shallow rise and fall of her chest.
Looking at her properly for the first time, he guesses she
is about the same age as him. Mid-twenties, maybe.
Thirty at most. She is fair-skinned, her long hair a

streaky mustard blonde. The alcoholic fug that seems to be oozing from her pores makes him want to gag.

'Madam? *Madam*?' he says, reaching over and tapping her on the arm. 'We are here already.'

Abbas's eyes drift to where her pressed-together thighs met the hem of her green miniskirt. He forces himself to look away. A photo of his wife Miriam is Sellotaped to the sun visor above his head. He feels that if he looks at it right now he will see the flash of chastisement in her eyes. The last time he saw her, a little under a year ago as she waved him goodbye at the airport, those eyes had dimmed with sadness and she had worn a defeated look on her face, as if she was always going to have an absent husband. It is such a depressing thought that he rids his mind of it quickly.

He puffs out his cheeks, pulls up the handbrake and turns off the engine. The match at the cafe will be well underway by now. Shahid Afridi halfway to a century in the first test. He thinks of his Pakistani countrymen dressed in their shalwar kameez, gathered around the TV at the Rainbow Cafe, filling their stomachs with *chappatis* and tea.

Feeling thirsty at the thought of tea, he takes out a bottle of water from the glove compartment and drinks half its contents. He considers flicking a few drops at the woman's face, startling her into consciousness, but there appears in his mind a vision of her lashing out with her long red nails, stomping her spiky heels into his new seat covers. He wishes now that he hadn't picked her up in the first place. She was obviously drunk, the way she had practically fallen into his waiting cab, but The Palm

Jumeirah to Bur Dubai is a seventy dirham fare. Who can turn down such a sum these days? Europeans often tipped well too. Intoxication seemed to bring out their generous streak.

He switches the meter off, and turns the engine back on. Resignedly, he decides that there is nothing to do but leave the woman alone until she wakes of her own accord, and if that takes until sunrise, so be it.

Abbas leaves his cab in a half-empty parking lot and walks the short distance to the cafe. The smell of *sheesha* smoke and a medley of mouth-watering spices hangs heavy in the cool February air. Though he has just put on an extra shirt he finds himself shivering.

As ever, most of the men sit outside the cafe on plastic chairs sipping cardamom-sweetened tea. Some eat piping hot chapattis from paper plates flimsy with grease. On any given night up to fifty men can be found huddled around the TV at the Rainbow Cafe. If there is no cricket then the wizened owner plays Bollywood films or soap operas. The camaraderie is always pleasant and it eases the homesickness – or is it lovesickness? – that often seizes Abbas's body like a fever.

Abbas notices a man in the crowd beckoning him over. It is Naseem, a cab driver in his late fifties who, like him, comes from a village on the outskirts of Karachi. Abbas is glad to have a fellow *Karachiite* as an acquaintance but several drivers have warned him that Naseem is sleazy and devious and best given a wide berth. Abbas, though, prefers to judge people for himself and until now has detected little in the older man's character to give him cause for concern. Naseem, his mouth full of food, acknowledges Abbas's presence with a grunt, then spits on the ground beside him.

'You look tired, my friend,' Naseem says. He takes out a white handkerchief embroidered with tiny butterflies and dabs at his neck. Naseem seems to perspire whatever the weather. The pale-green shalwar kameez he wears when he is off duty is always covered in dark patches of sweat. This, together with his rotund body, makes him look, thinks Abbas, like a giant, badly bruised apple.

Naseem points at the TV screen accusingly. 'Pakistan is 4 for 42,' he says. 'Afridi, the muthafucker, he's useless today.'

He rubs two fingers together in Abbas's face and arches an eyebrow. 'You have something for me, yes?'

Abbas blushes, remembering that he owes Naseem 100 dirhams from the previous month. It had been Miriam's birthday and he wanted to send home a little extra so she could replace the broken TV in their apartment, maybe buy a new sari.

'May I give it to you another time?' Abbas says. 'It's been a bad week. I'm sorry, Naseem.'

Naseem gives a wheezy sort of laugh. 'You work like a donkey and *still* you borrow? Look at Salim.' He points to a young guy nearby, conspicuous among the cafe crowd in that he is completely clean shaven. 'A cab driver, too, but always he has money and each night he has hanky-panky with a pretty little whore in Hor Al Anz.'

Abbas shrugs. 'Salim is unmarried and has few responsibilities.'

'Maybe,' Naseem says, 'But every man must ensure his sex needs are attended to. Tell me, Abbas, when is the last time you saw this beautiful wife you often speak of?'

Abbas doesn't feel comfortable talking about his wife in this way, especially to Naseem, but he doesn't want to start an argument. 'Eleven months ago. You know that, Naseem,' he says, feeling as though some anatomical alchemist has turned his heart into lead.

Naseem shakes his head, tuts and spits once more. They sit quietly watching the match. Abbas keeps glancing over at his cab in case the girl should suddenly wake up. He has parked the cab where he can keep an eye on it, has left the doors unlocked, the windows open. If the police come along they can hardly accuse him of abduction.

After a few minutes, Naseem begins to crack bawdy jokes, most of which Abbas has already heard from other drivers. When Naseem runs out of jokes, Abbas, who feels obliged to reciprocate with something humorous himself, decides to tell him about his passenger.

'Sleeping, huh?' Naseem says, before hawking up a ball of phlegm and leaning forward to expectorate onto the pavement. For a second it looks as though his head is tethered to the floor by a thin mucal stem.

'Like a baby,' Abbas says.

'And smelling of drink, you say?'

'Europeans... it's like medicine for them, I often think.'

Naseem tweaks at his groin and shifts in his chair. 'And what of her tits,' he says, cupping his own, not insubstantial, breasts. 'Are they juicy like the plumpest mangoes?'

'Sohail just hit a six,' Abbas says, pointing to the TV screen. He wishes he hadn't mentioned the woman to Naseem. He starts to feel deeply uncomfortable.

'Perhaps I may see her for myself?' Naseem says, his grin revealing nicotine-stained teeth. He is already on his feet and walking toward the parking lot before Abbas can protest. Naseem moves quickly for a fat man and by the time Abbas catches up with him he has almost reached the cab.

The parking lot is now empty but for two emaciated cats noisily contesting the rights to a half-eaten chicken drumstick. Naseem aims a kick at one of them and it scampers to safety, emitting a disgruntled mewl. Looking in through the cab's open back window, Naseem gives a shrill whistle of approval. The girl lies as before, but her skirt has ridden up her thighs, exposing lacy white underwear.

The two men stand still for a few seconds, as if contemplating an unfathomable piece of modern art. Somewhere near Dhiyafah Street a police siren can be heard getting louder and louder, reaching a crescendo near the fire station. Not until the sound has faded away do the men dare move again.

'I can't leave her like this,' Abbas says. Looking around nervously, he pushes Naseem out of the way, opens the back door and begins to unbutton his extra shirt.

'Wait!' Naseem says. 'Won't you let an old man take the first bite of the fruit?'

Abbas spins around to the sight of Naseem pulling up his shalwar kameez revealing a semi-erect penis beneath a hideously protruding belly.

'What the hell do you think you are doing, Naseem?'

'Sleeping beauties must be kissed by a handsome prince, no?' Naseem whispers. 'Or in this case' – he gives Abbas's bicep a friendly squeeze with his free hand – 'fucked by *two* handsome princes.'

Abbas turns his back on Naseem and takes off his shirt. He drapes it over the woman as if laying a lace tablecloth, delicately tugging at the corners so that it covers her from collarbone to calf. He sweeps behind her ear a lock of hair that obstructs her half-open mouth. Gently, quietly, he closes the door of the cab, then turns around to stand sentry-like before Naseem, who is no longer smiling.

'OK. No problem,' Naseem says. 'If you want to take the slut to my place that's perfectly—'

'I'm not taking her anywhere,' Abbas snaps. 'Have you lost your mind?'

'Look at her clothes,' Naseem says. 'A whore for sure. Do you think she's going to pay her fare?' A sly smile spreads across his face. 'We could forget about that hundred dirhams.'

'You'll get your money, Naseem,' Abbas says. 'Now put your prick away before those cats see it. They'll just as well fight over a maggot as a chicken bone.'

Back at the cafe, the men sit side by side watching the cricket, hostility creeping into the silence between them.

'I was making a joke,' Naseem says after a while. 'Was

that not obvious? By God, you're a dry one, Abbas Ali Khan.'

Abbas cannot make up his mind whether or not Naseem was joking. If he was, he cannot see anything funny in it, but when Naseem brings him a cup of tea as a peace offering he decides to give him the benefit of the doubt.

'Listen, as soon as you have money you should come with Salim and I to a little place we know in Hor Al Anz,' Naseem says. 'All work and no hanky-panky is most unhealthy for a man in the prime of his life. Your disposition is not good. You are ill-tempered, highly strung. You need to loosen up. Live a little, yes?' He takes several sips of his tea. 'Here,' he says, digging into his pocket. 'I want to show you something.'

Naseem takes out his wallet and hands Abbas several pictures of a naked Ethiopian woman in various poses. Abbas is surprised by her lithe beauty, her bright eyes and clear skin. She wears the same shy look on her face as Miriam did on her wedding night. It had been the first time for both of them. In the morning he had asked her if she liked it and she had nodded, avoiding his eyes, as though it was shameful to do so. They had talked about that night only last week on the phone, the sound of her voice driving him mad with the need for her. Sometimes, when long-haired Asian women got into the passenger seat beside him, he yearned to reach out and wrap his fingers in their tresses, smell it, push his face into it. Not that he would ever dare. Checking that no one but Naseem can see them, he studies the pictures. The Ethiopian's physical perfection makes them almost tasteful, artistic. The street girls he used to see walking the back streets of Karachi were so different, dead-eyed, their faces pock-marked and pitiful. He finds himself becoming aroused.

'How old is this girl?' Abbas asks.

'Twenty two,' Naseem says. 'When I am with her, I too am feeling twenty-two again.' He laughs gleefully, slaps Abbas's back so hard that he makes him spill his tea. Abbas forces a tight smile.

'Oh, come on! You are not even tempted?' Naseem winks. 'She has many friends.'

'I am sure,' Abbas says. 'But this kind of thing... it is not for me.'

Three months previously, a Chinese prostitute who couldn't afford to pay her cab fare had made an obscene gesture to Abbas. She spoke no English and it took him a moment to realise she was making him an offer of services in lieu of money. He had politely declined and gave her his mobile phone number, told her to call him when she had the money, but she never did. He wonders now what he would do if such a thing happened again.

His thoughts drift to Miriam. She had defied her parents' wishes by marrying him instead of a wealthier suitor. To cheat on her, he thinks, would be to irrevocably taint the purity of their relationship. Morally, he considers himself superior to men like Naseem and Salim. He is a good and decent man. That is why Miriam agreed to marry him. Despite his penury, he is, she once told him, her king, 'sent from Heaven itself, and filled with a goodness rare in men'. When she had said these words, he'd felt bathed by a warm glow of gratitude, knew in the very core of his heart that he would always be faithful to her.

Now, though, he has to admit that certain urges are getting harder to ignore. Eleven months he has been in Dubai without once returning home. Eleven months spent stuck in the city's traffic jams, breathing in the fetid air of perspiring passengers, putting up with their abuse, their insistence on fiddling with the switches on his stereo because they hate 'that bloody Bollywood racket', their clueless directions barked at him in dozens of strange accents and languages that they somehow expect Abbas, a man with little formal education, to understand.

The previous week one of his colleagues, a man of barely forty, had been forced to take early retirement after failing a medical test. The word amongst the other drivers was that he was suffering from respiratory problems caused by decades of sitting in an air-conditioned cab for up to fourteen hours a day. Is that what he, Abbas, could look forward to also? By the time he has earned enough money to set up his own business back in Karachi, he might be an invalid, unable to work, let alone satisfy his wife.

Maybe Naseem is right, he thinks. A little harmless carnal pleasure will release some tension. He has never been one for meals in fancy restaurants. He hates the taste of alcohol and abhors nightclubs with their deafening music and smoky air, even if he could afford such pleasures. As for the Bollywood films he sometimes watches, their corny boy-gets-girl endings always make him feel more depressed and alone.

He looks again at the photographs of the prostitute and hands them back to Naseem.

'This place in Hor Al Anz?' Abbas says. 'Where is it?'

Naseem wheezes with laughter and a few people in the cafe turn to look at them. 'Good man,' he says. 'Call me tomorrow night, we'll arrange something.'

When Abbas gets back to his cab it is almost 6 a.m. and he is so tired he can scarcely keep his eyes open. He decides he can no longer wait for the woman to wake up, so he opens the back door and lightly shakes her ankle.

'Madam,' he says, pleadingly. 'Madam. You must wake up now. *Please.*'

She makes a low groaning sound and, eventually, her eyes flutter open. Lifting her head slightly and struggling to focus on Abbas, who is standing outside the cab holding the door open, she touches her head and grimaces. She sits up and looks out of the window, then gazes curiously down at Abbas's shirt crumpled in her lap.

'Mine,' Abbas says. 'It was so cold.'

The woman studies Abbas's face, narrowing her eyes, as if he is someone whose name she might remember if she tries hard enough.

'I am your taxi driver,' Abbas says. 'When we reached your destination you would not wake.'

The woman appears to check herself, as if she has just plummeted down the face of a cliff and can scarcely believe that nothing has been broken. She retrieves a small silver purse which has fallen onto the floor of the cab and checks its contents, giving it a discreet squeeze. She fingers the gold watch on her wrist.

Satisfied that everything is in order – nothing stolen, nothing violated – her body slackens with relief. She lets her head loll against the back of the seat and closes her eyes.

'What place is this?' she slurs. Her voice has a harsh rasping quality that makes Abbas think of stroking snake scales against the grain.

'We are in Satwa,' Abbas says, closing the back door and walking around to the front of the cab. He gets in and puts on his seatbelt.

'Listen, I need to get home,' the woman says. She wraps her arms around herself and brings a pair of bruised knees up to her chest. 'Can you take me there? Rolla Street. I live on Rolla Street. Do you know it?'

'Yes,' Abbas says. 'I know it.' When they get to Rolla Street the woman gives Abbas a hundred dirham note, tells him to keep the change. Abbas protests, but she insists, pushing his hand away.

Before she gets out of the cab, the woman asks, 'So, like, how long was I asleep?'

'Oh, hours,' Abbas says. 'If the sky rained elephants it would not have woken you.'

'Friend's birthday, all got a bit messy,' the woman says. 'Christ, this is embarrassing. I've never done this before.'

Abbas doesn't know what to say so he just smiles.

'Suppose I should count myself lucky,' the woman says.

'Lucky?'

'Some real creeps out there.'

'Creeps?' Abbas says. 'What is creeps?'

The woman laughs. 'Sort of like, bad men, I suppose.'

Abbas nods. 'Yes,' he says. 'Too many creeps we have in Dubai.'

The woman sits forward and checks her reflection in the rear view mirror. She tidies up her hair. Sticking her head through the gap in the seats, she kisses Abbas on the cheek and squeezes his shoulder.

'Bye then,' she says. 'You're a nice guy. But then I'm sure you've been told that before, right?'

The Abu Dhabi Brass Rubbing Society

Rowan finished replacing the flat tyre and watched as the chopper approached. It was red with bright yellow skids, a curlicue of white Arabic script on the boom tail. A minute ago it had been a wasp-sized dot creeping across the expanse of their windscreen; now it was hovering over them like a bird of prey, the *wanga-wanga* throb of its rotor blades drowning out Bonnie Tyler on the stereo.

'What on earth is that helicopter doing?' shouted Leila. She was sitting in the front passenger seat blowing on freshly-painted fingernails.

'Damned if I know,' replied Rowan. 'Stay in the car.'

He felt certain it was the same chopper they had seen earlier skimming the peaks of the mountain range that ran parallel to the highway. And hadn't they heard a helicopter pass over the petrol station in Jumeirah that morning? Come to think of it, one had flown so low over their backyard the other week that it had shaken the pods off the tamarind tree. Their neighbours, the nice Iranian couple whose names they could never remember, thought they might be looking for bank robbers, but nobody robbed banks here. Nobody ever seemed to rob anything.

Recalling the previous night at the Mugford's villa in Abu Dhabi, he found himself mentally assessing each participant's potential for indiscretion. Two of the couples they had known from the scene back in England, but the third, Lisa and Jeremy Cahill, were first-timers. They had taken a gamble in allowing them to join the group. She seemed level-headed enough, but he was a loud-mouthed braggart.

One loose word in the wrong company, that's all it would take, and their whole world would come crashing down around them. They had it good out here. Tax-free salary, warm weather, a palatial villa that was the envy of their cooped-up London friends. Rowan often wondered whether it was worth the risk, and the answer, until now, was invariably yes. The 'gatherings', as Leila euphemistically called them, gave them something to look forward to at weekends, especially in summer when it was too hot to go outside. God knows they had had their fill of traipsing around sterile shopping malls and lounging around the swimming pool on the compound with a bunch of smug wankers who droned on and on about what a dump Britain had become since they left, as if their departure alone had put a dent in the country's kudos.

Shielding his eyes from the sun, Rowan craned his

neck upwards to get a good look at the chopper. This is what it must feel like to be a helpless field mouse about to be swooped on, hauled away to some mountain-top eyrie and torn to shreds. Feeling his knees begin to buckle, he placed one hand on the trunk of the car to steady himself and breathed slowly and deeply. Maybe the Mugford's neighbours had somehow cottoned on. They too were Brits, but older, straight-laced. That rare breed of veteran expat – lifers, Rowan called them – who kowtowed to the culture, spoke a bit of the lingo, kissed the locals' arses so that their business interests ran more smoothly. Had they called the police? Maybe they thought there were drugs involved. It didn't make any sense, the chopper landing out here in this vast expanse of nothingness. They *must* have followed them here to arrest them, way out in the desert where there were no witnesses. Spirit them away to some hellish prison nobody knew about. It would be days before anyone realised they had gone. That's what they did in these countries, wasn't it? Torture a confession out of you before they let you see a lawyer? He'd read all about it in a newspaper – a German man in Saudi or Kuwait, banged up for fifteen years for brewing illegal hooch.

The chopper was descending now. Rowan could make out two men in the cabin: the pilot, in a blue shirt with black epaulettes, and his passenger, a man in a white *kandora*. Before he could get a proper look at them the chopper began to sway violently from side to side. When it was about twenty feet from the ground, its nose dipped and Rowan could only watch, helpless, as it disappeared behind a large sand dune. He half expected to see a mushroom of flame shoot into the clear blue sky. Instead there came a dull thud, followed by an earthly tremor that tickled the soles of his feet.

By the time he had run over the dune the two men were walking away from the chopper. To Rowan's guilty disappointment it was intact, save for one of the skids, which had buckled. He felt like a Death Row prisoner who has been given a reprieve, only to find out seconds later that it was a clerical error and that his execution has instead been brought forward. He anxiously watched their approach.

The man in the *kandora* was resting an arm on the pilot's shoulder to take the weight off his right leg and his head was bleeding. He was blandly handsome, more Mediterranean than Arabian in appearance, and his beard looked like a dusting of iron filings. The pilot resembled a fat Omar Sharif in aviator shades.

'He's okay but he should see a doctor,' said the pilot.

Rowan asked him where the nearest hospital was and the pilot pointed in the direction they had come from.

'I will stay here, with the helicopter,' said the pilot. 'Help is coming. Please, you must take care of my friend. Khalil, his name is Khalil.'

On the way to the hospital Leila sat with Khalil in the back seat tending to his wounds. His ankle had begun to swell and there was a small gash in his forehead. She used wet wipes to clean the wound as best she could. Using nail scissors from her make-up bag she cut off a strip of beach towel for a tourniquet.

'Leila is an Arabic name,' said Khalil as Leila gently

wound the strip of towel around his head. For the life of him Rowan couldn't recall any introductions taking place. He tried to remember if he had used his wife's name when they had helped Khalil into the car.

'Yes,' said Leila. 'My father's Lebanese.'

'*Christian*-Lebanese,' Rowan blurted out before he could stop himself. Somebody at work had told him that some Arab men didn't like their women *talking* to Western males, never mind marrying them. As for allowing them to participate in the kind of activities more commonly associated with debauched Roman emperors, well, that was like *asking* to be stoned to death. 'Born in England, weren't you, my love?' he added for good measure. 'Not very Arabic at all really. Not that that there's anything wrong with that. I mean—'

Leila shot him a look that said, '*Shut. Up.*' so he did.

Khalil laughed and Rowan studied his face in the rear view mirror, searching for a clue. Genuine amusement, or the sort of gleeful chuckle emitted by a Bond villain before he lowers 007 into the shark-infested tank? It was impossible to tell.

An archipelago of blood ran shoulder to waist down Khalil's *kandora* and a claret smear had found its way onto the passenger seat. Rowan silently cursed his wife for persuading him to take the white leather option – 'It's not like we've got any kids to clean up after,' she had said to the sales guy in the showroom. Rowan had been perfectly happy with grey velour.

'So what happened back there?' Rowan asked Khalil when his wife had finished patching him up.

'Maybe mechanical failure,' said Khalil. 'We were forced into emergency landing.'

'Where were you headed?'

'To Hatta. To visit a cousin.' There was a flatness to Khalil's voice, as if he was reading off an autocue.

'I thought you were coming from the other direction,' said Rowan, trying to keep an accusatory tone out of his voice. 'I thought I saw you earlier, up near the mountains?'

'*Rowan*,' said Leila, hardly moving her mouth.

'Sorry,' said Khalil. 'Maybe I, uh, not understand question.'

'Always travel by helicopter do you?' said Rowan, tapping the steering wheel to an absent beat. 'When visiting family, I mean?'

'Please, I...' Khalil gestured to his head.

Leila jabbed her knee into the back of Rowan's seat.

'Sorry,' said Rowan. 'I didn't mean to pry... Just get some rest. We're nearly there.'

When they reached the hospital Khalil was taken into A&E in a wheelchair by an Indian nurse who pushed him down a long corridor and through a set of floppy red double doors.

'Let's get out of here,' said Rowan, his hand on the small of Leila's back, manoeuvring her toward the exit.

'Just leave him?' asked Leila, standing firm. 'That's rude. No, we're staying until we know he's alright. *Alright*?'

Leila laughed and shook her head. 'You were like the Spanish Inquisition back there, Ro,' she said. 'As if the poor guy's head wasn't already pounding.'

Rowan glanced around the room. 'Leila. I think...' He took a step closer to his wife. 'I think he's the police.'

'You're being paranoid'

'They've been following us. I've got a bad feeling about this.'

'Why, Rowan, why would they follow *us*?'

'Why do you think?' hissed Rowan. 'The *gatherings*. They're on to us.'

She rolled her eyes. 'You're imagining things.'

'I don't think so, Leila.'

'But we're discreet, how could they possibly know?'

'Nosy neighbours peeping through the curtains, that bloody Cahill guy shooting his mouth off... Christ, I'm gonna be sick.'

Clutching his stomach, Rowan ran to find the toilets. When he returned ashen-faced several minutes later, Leila had bought two cups of watery tea from a vending machine. Rowan saw her fiddle with the ethnic bangle on her wrist and knew that Leila was now worried too.

'How are you feeling?' she said.

Rowan shrugged and sat down next to Leila on one of the waiting room's red plastic chairs. Apart from three young Asian women at the reception desk, they were the only people there.

'I've been thinking,' said Leila, handing him one of the polystyrene cups. 'We ought to make sure our stories are the same. Just in case.'

'We'll say it's a poker tournament,' said Rowan.

'But that's gambling!'

'A film club then. We watch foreign movies on a cinescreen. That's why we draw the curtains.'

'What if they raid our DVD collection?' said Leila. 'Those films you bought in Amsterdam.'

'I don't know... flamin' brass rubbing then,' said Rowan, tugging the hair on the back of his neck. 'We're the Abu Dhabi Brass Rubbing Society. Oh, what does it matter? Frankly, Leila, I think we're fucked.'

Rowan took a sip of his tea and grimaced.

'This,' he said,' tastes like piss.

After an hour, Khalil emerged from a door beyond the reception of the A&E room. His head was properly bandaged and he was using a crutch to help him walk.

'You are still here,' he said. 'This makes me very happy.'

I bet it does, thought Rowan. He thought he was going to puke again. He gripped Leila's hand, realised he hadn't held it so tightly since they were on the roller coaster at Alton Towers – their first proper date. Fitting really, since these were probably their last moments together outside of a courtroom for years.

'Come, please,' said Khalil, urging them to follow him as he limped to the entrance of the hospital.

Muted by the heat, they stood waiting outside in silence as the rays of the afternoon sun bore down on them. Rowan felt sweat run down his forehead and fill the pores and shallow wrinkles of his face. It was as though every hair follicle on his head was being cauterised with the accuracy of laser surgery. Right now, he despised this fucking country. Its stifling weather, its people, its draconian laws. He despised it so much that if someone had given him a button to nuke it there and then, blow it to kingdom come, he would have happily obliged. He watched Khalil pull a mobile out of his pocket and read a text message. Again, Rowan studied his face for some kind of sign, but Khalil was as difficult to read as Arabic scripture itself.

Rowan thought he was about to pass out from heat exhaustion when a white Mercedes pulled up in front of them with a screech. A man in a *kandora* leapt out of the back door and ran to Khalil, embracing him and speaking in breathless Arabic. After he had helped Khalil into the car he approached Leila and Rowan with what looked like gratitude on his face. For the first time since the chopper had landed, Rowan imagined himself watching that evening's sunset from the beach in Khor Fakkan with an ice cream in his hand, rather than through the barred windows of a cockroach-infested prison cell.

'My brother tells me you may have a small cleaning bill to take care of.' The man pressed something into the pit of Rowan's palm. 'This, I trust, will cover it.'

And then the two men were gone, the caustic bile of fear draining out of Rowan as quickly as the sweet stream of relief poured in. He looked at Leila, who was staring open-mouthed at the Mercedes as it disappeared in a swirling fug of sulphuric-looking yellow dust. It made Rowan think of the special effects in an *Aladdin* pantomime he had once seen.

Looking down at the roll of bank notes he held in his hand, Rowan peeled off the top one, damp from his clammy palm, and held it up to the sun.

They were back in the car and heading, at last, for the

117

coast, when Leila finished counting the money. 'Twenty seven thousand dirhams!' she said, scrutinising one of the big blue notes for the umpteenth time, unable to believe they were real.

'Suppose it's a drop in the ocean for some of these Arabs,' she continued. 'Probably carries that around with him just to wipe his backside. Here, do you reckon he was a sheikh?'

'Who knows?' said Rowan.

'We could buy one of those king-size waterbeds with this,' said Leila. 'Lisa Mugford said that—'

'Maybe we should stay away from the Mugfords and their parties for a while,' interrupted Rowan. 'It's too risky.' He reached for the wiper switch to move a dead leaf that had got stuck on the windscreen and realised that his hands were trembling.

'A holiday then,' said Leila. 'We haven't been home in almost a year.'

'I don't know why you pine for home the way you do,' said Rowan. 'We've got it pretty good here, Leila, you've got to admit.'

'I know, but there's a gathering next month at that old rectory in Kent. That McCormack couple, you know the Scottish ones with the outdoor Jacuzzi? They're organising it.'

Rowan took a deep breath and exhaled slowly through his nose.

'Oh, darling,' said Leila. 'Don't turn all prude on me.'

She ran a crimson fingernail along the top of Rowan's thigh and laughed. It was a sound Rowan had once found a turn on, an instant and infallible cock-stirrer, but not now. He turned on the stereo and tuned in to one of the English-language stations. Justin Bieber would never sound this good again.

As he fixed his eyes on the long, unwinding road ahead, it occurred to him that spending the weekends traipsing around shopping malls and sitting by the swimming pool with a bunch of smug wankers wasn't such a bad thing after all.

The Adidas Amulet

Marcus and I are about to close up for the night when we hear an electronic bleep from one of the cross trainers in the corner, behind the partition that separates the machines from the free weights.

Marcus grunts as he lifts a stray dumbbell from the floor and slots it into a gap on the rack. 'Go on, Ramon,' he says, pronouncing my name 'ramen', like the noodles, even though I've told him a thousand times. 'You can evict her majesty this time.'

I head for the machine area where I know I will find the Emirati woman in the black *shayla* and white tracksuit. Since Ramadan ended two weeks ago she has turned up every Monday, Wednesday and Saturday evening. She stays until one of us – Marcus, Caroline or myself – politely informs her that it is closing time. She is young and quite plump. If she were one of the three body types illustrated on a chart on a nearby wall, she would be the one labelled 'endomorph' but she seems determined to stick to the carefully mapped out training program that Caroline has designed for her. Between sets she takes long rests and sits beside the water cooler scrolling through the tunes on her shiny pink iPod. As she does this she chews on a plastic toggle that dangles from a drawstring in the collar of her tracksuit top. It occurs to me that she may be on a diet and does this to keep hunger at bay.

I approach her from behind. The wall in front of where she exercises is mirrored, but she has her eyes closed and is unaware of my presence. She wears her iPod clipped to the waistband of her sweatpants and a set of chunky headphones over her scarf. I stand in front of her and recall my boss Lucas's lecture about practising caution when dealing with Muslim women. In particular we are not to make physical contact, even when correcting potentially harmful exercise techniques. This is not easy when you are a fitness trainer, but it is a rule I dare not break. Take for instance my former colleague Gaspar, who three months ago placed an innocent hand on the small of an Emirati lady's back when showing her how to perform a tricep extension. Her hysterical reaction suggested she had been the victim of a bag snatch. The woman's husband, who happened to be exercising nearby, slapped Gaspar across the face and demanded that Lucas fire him on the spot. Since the man was a government official and threatened to involve the police, Lucas had little choice but to submit to his request. Gaspar now washes dishes at some shithole three-star hotel in Ras al-Khaimah and struggles to pay off his car loan. As for me, I keep our female Arabic clients at arm's length. I like my job.

'Ma'am,' I say to the woman. 'Excuse me.' She has the music turned up so loud that I can hear it blaring out of her headphones. A different approach is needed so I rap my knuckles on the metal frame of the cross-trainer. Eventually she feels the vibrations and opens her eyes. She stops exercising and pulls the headphones down around her neck.

'Closing time already?' she asks, breathlessly. Her face has turned red and tiny sweat beads glisten above her top lip.

'Yes, Ma'am,' I say, pointing to the clock on the wall. 'It's ten o'clock.'

'Okay, no problem,' she says. She gets off the cross-trainer and reaches down for her water bottle on the floor.

'Always keep your back straight when you use the cross-trainer,' I say.

I see her eyebrows rise indignantly, and it occurs to me that what I just said may have sounded more like a command than a piece of friendly advice. Other nationalities – least of all Filipinos, who seem to be regarded by many Arabs as a servile race – do *not* issue commands to Emiratis.

'Then perhaps next time you can show me the correct way...' Her eyes narrow as she studies the name badge pinned to my polo shirt. '...Ramon Villanueva.'

Marcus and I jokingly refer to the Emirati woman as 'her majesty' because she drives to the gym in a gold-coloured Volkswagen Beetle and lays a little white towel over the seat of the exercise bike or the rowing machine or anything else she sits on, as though her perspiration is too precious to be transferred to the backsides of common folk. Of course, if she were genuine royalty she would have her own private gym in her palace and a personal trainer. She would not come to Health & Strength Ltd – though it is fair to say we are one of the more exclusive gyms in town. The next time I see her, though, she looks anything but majestic. It is a Monday night and she is laying into the punch bag, connecting with the heels of her small gloveless hands. I stand watching her for a minute, trying to keep a straight face, when she spots me.

'Hey there, Ramon Villanueva!' she says, putting her hands on her hips and turning from brute to beauty with a wide smile. 'You know how to fight, right? I have seen the way you beat this thing.'

It's true, I throw a few jabs at the bag when the gym isn't busy. Staff are not supposed to use the facilities during opening hours, but when you work with annoying people like Marcus all day you need an outlet for your frustration.

'Yes, Ma'am, I know karate and I did a little boxing back in the Philippines.'

'Then you can show me some moves,' she says.

Can you get into trouble, I wonder, for teaching a female Muslim how to throw a perfect right hook? Everyone knows that Sheikha Maitha, a member of the ruling family, won a silver medal in Tae Kwondo at the Asian Games a few years ago. But that's a Sheikha. Different rules apply.

I tell her about Emmanuel, a Nigerian guy who runs our Judo classes. He's a great instructor and Tuesday night is for women only so she wouldn't have to do anything *haram* like grapple on the mats with men.

'No, I want *you* to teach me,' she says. 'How to punch, how to kick. You know, the basics, yes?'

When I ask her why she wants to learn this stuff, she tells me she plans to enrol in the Emirates Police Academy, who are recruiting a new batch of female officers in six months' time. She wants to lose a couple of kilos, toughen up before attempting the training course.

We don't provide gloves for the punch bag so I fetch my own pair from the office. She doesn't even flinch, as I was certain she would, when she sees that the faded red leather is battered, and stiff with old sweat. I loosen the laces of the gloves so that they slip easily over her hands without my fingers brushing her skin. Then I tie them up, but not too tightly – I don't want to leave any marks.

Standing beside her in front of the mirror I demonstrate the correct positions for the feet and hands. I show her how to throw a straight punch. Then we go over to the bag and I stand behind it, holding it steady as she pounds away, grunting like a female tennis player and denting the canvas. After a couple of minutes she is panting for breath and almost everyone in the gym is pretending not to watch us.

'I think that's enough for today, Ma'am' I say, self-conscious of our growing audience.

'Alright,' she says. 'And please, Ramon, the

"Ma'am"... it is not necessary. You can call me Rana from now on. Okay?'

Three weeks later, Rana comes into the gym with a tall, slim man in a *kandora*. She sees me by the water cooler and heads toward me, man in tow.

'This is Omar, my husband,' says Rana. 'He wanted to meet you.'

Warily, I shake hands with Omar. He is in his mid-forties and sports a greying, neatly-trimmed goatee beard. His *kandora* looks comically out of place in the gym. Flawlessly clean and creaseless amidst the dishevelled cotton tracksuits stained with fresh sweat.

Omar is pleasant and relaxed, if a little reluctant to offer me a smile. He doesn't seem the type to slap anyone.

'You teach my wife very good,' he says. 'I tell her, Filipino guy, no problem. I trust Filipinos. Good people. Our cleaner is from Mindinao.' Rana gives me an embarrassed, apologetic smile, and heads for the treadmill.

Of course I know what Omar is *really* saying. He is saying that an Emirati woman could never be attracted to a lowly Filipino and therefore I am not a sexual threat in the way that a Western man, or perhaps even another Arab would be. This is why he has allowed his wife to be coached by me. It has little to do with trust or goodness. Despite my annoyance, I manage not to show it. I'm sure he doesn't mean to patronise me.

He keeps glancing about the gym, eyeing the equipment. I ask him whether he is interested in becoming a member, but he says he doesn't have the time. The clang of clashing dumbbells and physical exertions ring out around us. Everyone in the room is totally focused on their exercises.

Perhaps Omar was expecting a place full of vain young gigolos. He seems satisfied, however, that it is a respectable establishment dedicated solely to physical advancement. 'There are other… uh,' he searches for the word. '…instructors?'

I point to Caroline and Marcus, who are both attending to clients in the free weights area. 'There are three of us, sir,' I say. He studies Marcus, decides, perhaps, that he is too big-eared to be attractive to even the most desperate spinster, and gives a satisfied nod. 'Okay, *habibi*, very nice to meet you,' he says to me, and gives Rana a little wave goodbye before leaving the gym. I look out of the window and watch him drive off in a black Toyota Land Cruiser with mirror-tinted windows.

Later, I approach Rana as she sits beside the water cooler, chewing thoughtfully on a toggle. I ask her what her husband does. She goes into the little sports bag she always carries around with her and hands me a business card that says:

Omar Al Badari,
Equine Homeopath

I tell her I'm not sure what this means, so she explains that he works for one of the sheikhs, treating his race horses with natural medicines. A ripple of anxiety passes through my body. Omar clearly has friends in high places.

Rana starts to come to the gym more often. So does Omar. It is against the rules for non-members to hang around the way he does, but everyone, even Lucas, is afraid to say anything, especially since I told them what Omar does for a living. He never stays long, anyway. Just stands around in his *kandora* and white Birkenstock sandals, looking serious and making calls on his mobile phone. His presence at the gym makes me uncomfortable. I try to avoid conversing with him because he always says the same thing to me. 'Filipinos good people. Hard working.' I try to look grateful, as though he has pinned a medal to my chest, but sometimes my face actually aches from the fake-smiling.

One day he asks me if anyone in my family is looking for a job. His Pakistani house-keeper is retiring soon. Do I know anyone, a relative maybe, who might be interested in replacing him for a salary of three thousand dirhams a month? By the look on his face it is obvious that he expects me to be impressed by this figure, a fraction of my salary. I tell him no, I am an only child from a small family and my parents are retired (both lies). I do not tell him that we own a clothes shop in a mall in Metro Manila and that we are, if not exactly rich, far from poor. Unlike the vast majority of my *kabayans* I did not come to Dubai for money but to be closer to my wife, a secretary at the Philippines Embassy in Abu Dhabi, and our seven-year-old son.

By the end of January Rana has shed almost two kilos in body weight. When she lays into the punch bag she is like a woman possessed. I tell her to take it easy. The leather on my old gloves is wearing thin and I worry about her damaging her knuckles, breaking a finger. One night I have a dream in which Rana injures herself so badly that Omar punishes me by burying me up to my neck in the desert, urinating on my head and abandoning me to the sun and the scorpions.

One Monday evening, I'm standing over by the bench press, casually trading nutrition tips with a client, when I see Rana, who has been resting beside the water cooler, stand up and clutch her throat. Even from several metres away I can see that the expression on her face is a mixture of fear and panic.

I run over and she takes a faltering step toward me. She tries to tell me something but nothing comes out.

'Are you choking?' I ask her, though it feels ridiculous to even ask. 'Nod if you are.'

She nods vigorously.

I turn around to look for Caroline but she is nowhere to be seen and Marcus has the day off. My prayers that some other woman will step in and save the day go unanswered. Almost everyone in the gym has stopped what they are doing and is watching the scene unfold.

A red-haired Danish woman steps into my vision, shoots me a look of disgust and disbelief. 'Of course she's choking you idiot!' she says. 'Don't just stand there, do something. Don't you know first aid?'

Rana sinks to her knees in front of me and I hear a woman behind me saying 'Oh my God!'

'CAROLINE!' I shout, but she must be in the downstairs toilet.

The Danish woman pulls out a mobile. 'I can't believe this,' she says, shaking her head and frantically dialling a number. 'A gym where no one knows first aid? *Unbelievable*!'

But she is wrong. I do know first aid. I know CPR and can shoot a diabetic with insulin. I can deal with an epileptic fit and ease an attack of cramp with massage. What I *cannot* do is wrap myself around a female Muslim. Grope around for her navel and her rib-cage. Shunt her upwards, my groin pressing into her back, to unblock her trachea, and *that* – namely the Heimlich manoeuvre – is what is required here. I find myself in a circle of expectant faces that seems to close in on us – Rana and I – with every passing second. Her lips have not yet started to turn blue, but any second now this will change.

She looks up at me with pleading and desperation in her eyes and I know that this face will forever be etched into my mind if she doesn't make it. Whatever the consequences, I cannot stand by and do nothing. So I move behind her, lift her to her feet and do what I have to do. It takes several, undignified shunts before the obstruction is expelled from her mouth. I watch it arc through the air, hit the wooden floor and roll under the dumbbell rack.

Rana collapses to a heap on the floor and takes down big gulps of air, her mouth wide open. Relief and the fear of the inevitable repercussions wash over me as I recall the story I once read about a French Muslim attacking his wife's male gynecologist who had stepped in to help with a complicated delivery.

Rana's breathing regains some sort of normality and I move her into the recovery position. I hear someone tell the grumbling Danish woman that the reason she hasn't been able to call an ambulance is because she has been dialling 911. The emergency services number in the UAE is 999. Who's the idiot now?

I sit with Rana and Caroline in the office at the back of the gym. Caroline makes Rana chamomile and honey tea to soothe her throat and urges her to go to hospital for a check up, but she refuses. She doesn't want Omar, who is expecting her home soon, to know what happened. Neither do I, but deep down I am also disappointed that he will never know that I saved his wife's life.

After an hour, Rana drives herself home. Before she goes we tell her to take a week off, she's had a nasty shock, but she insists she'll be okay in a day or two. Caroline and I shrug our shoulders. There is nothing we can do.

At closing time, when we are tidying up and switching off the lights, I go over to the dumbbell rack and retrieve the offending item. As I expected, it is the plastic toggle from Rana's tracksuit. It is black and about the size of a cherry. I wipe it on my T-shirt, wrap it in a paper towel and put it in my pocket.

When Rana turns up alone the following Wednesday she is wearing the Adidas tracksuit with the missing toggle. Its lonely twin dangles from one end of her collar. She spends several minutes thanking me for what I did, and then says that it's best not to talk about it again, even though she can never repay me for saving her life. I tell her it was nothing, to forget about it and just concentrate on her training from now on. She is doing well. She'll be top of her class at the police academy, outperforming even her male colleagues.

'Here, take this,' I say, giving her the toggle. 'They should be reunited.'

She laughs when she realises what it is and hands it back to me, taking my fingers and wrapping them around the toggle. Her hands are warm, her skin surprisingly rough.

'You keep it, Ramon,' she says. 'Think of it as an amulet which will bring you luck – such things work, believe me.'

So I attach it to the bunch of car keys I always carry around, thinking: what's lucky about an object that nearly killed someone? But the thing is, it *does* give me a strange feeling of power when I reach into my pocket and squeeze it between finger and thumb. A power that is at its most potent when Omar strolls into the gym, pats me on the head, and says in that condescending way of his: 'Filipinos good people. Very nice. Very friendly.'

Wind Chimes

The wind chimes wake me up again. Every night they straddle the remnants of my dreams and the first woozy seconds after re-joining the real world, sweat-soaked and dry-mouthed.

My watch on the bedside table reads 11.51 p.m. – exactly four hours slow because I can't bear to change it to the local time. This way I can almost convince myself that I'm on an extended holiday, not stuck in Dubai for God knows how long thanks to Danielle's big-bucks promotion and inexorable surge up the career ladder.

Danielle doubts they exist, swears she's never even heard them. Not that she'd know. She sleeps like a hibernating bear until her alarm clock goes off, and then it's at least a dozen antagonistic bleeps before she reaches out her arm and slaps the snooze button. She's convinced I'm suffering from some kind of post-traumatic stress disorder brought on by the suddenness of the move – we arrived from the UK just two months ago with minimal preparation or planning – but I'm certain they're as real as the air I breathe.

I can never figure out where the sound comes from. Usually it stops before I get the chance, but tonight it lingers, a delicate wisp of a sound, creeping ever closer. For several minutes I lie in bed, eyes wide open, listening to it. I have the urge to shake Danielle awake, but she needs her rest for some early morning business meeting in Abu Dhabi. Besides, I first want proof that it's not a figment of my troubled mind. I want to seek out the source, find evidence so I can prove to her that, no actually, I am *not* 'losing the fucking plot'.

I get out of bed, still wearing the shorts and T-shirt I fell asleep in, and put on a pair of sandals. I drink a glass of water in the kitchen then go into the lounge and slide open the doors to the balcony. I shiver when I step out into the cool, still air – not just from the drop in temperature but because of what I see. Or rather, don't see because of the preternaturally dense fog that has draped itself over the city. The winter months bring to the Arabian deserts these low-hanging pea-soupers, chiffon-thick like Jack the Ripper's London. Like an ancient mariner's nightmare.

To the left of me, just out of sight unless I take a precarious bow over the railing of my balcony and crane my neck around, is Sheikh Zayed Road, a long domino row of half-lit skyscrapers. In front of me and to my right there is only the desert. Not a landscape, to my mind, but the dry bones of one, ground by the mortar and pestle of time into microscopic grains. Dead, all of it. I can't imagine ever loving it the way I do the forested hills of home, which I long for more than anything, including Danielle's love for me, which seems to diminish by the day.

On the balcony, the washed clothes I put out that afternoon hang still as icicles from the rungs of the dryer. Not even the faintest breeze stirs in the air, but I can still hear the wind chimes. Maybe someone is moving them. An insomniac neighbour, perhaps. A DJ or a surgeon. Someone whose work finishes when the rest of us have long gone to bed.

I'm gazing out into the murky abyss when I hear them louder than I've ever heard them before. So tantalisingly close now that I feel they'd be visible were it not for the fog. They seem to be coming from somewhere on the ground, not a neighbour's balcony as I first thought. Wind chimes, or bells? Maybe bells. It feels as though someone is willing me to find them, sating at last my gnawing curiosity.

So as not to wake Danielle, I insert myself into my jeans and T-shirt as carefully as if I were stepping into hot bath water, then I head out, leaving the apartment door unlocked. In the lobby the security guard nods at me as I pass him, a puzzled look on his bearded face.

Once outside, I stand still for a moment and listen. A couple of cars whoosh by on the road in front of the building, followed by something heavier, clanking away, and then I hear it again. Bells, definitely. Not the iron bells of clock towers or churches, however, but the tiny bells of a leper's ankle or a jester's hat.

I walk to the far end of the car park at the rear of the

building and step up on to on the low perimeter wall, the brickwork so greasily damp that I almost slip. Willing my eyes to find some way through the fog and the darkness, I can just about discern the outline of the large dune ahead of me that I've noticed in the daytime. Its shape changes imperceptibly week by week, sculpted by the whim of the wind, but its size remains constant. Behind it, I'm sure, lies the source of the sound.

I remove my sandals, the sand loose and cool on the soles of my feet, and trudge forward, breathing heavily, the condensation pouring out of my nostrils getting swallowed instantly by the fog as though it wants a taste of me. As I ascend the dune it becomes more difficult, steeper. Sand cascades over the tops of my feet, temporarily burying them, and I find myself worrying about unseen scorpions. For every three laboured steps I take I slide back one. When I feel like I'm quite high up, I turn around and see that I am at eye level with my apartment on the third floor. I wish Danielle would come to the window right now and look out, but maybe she wouldn't see me through the thick fog. Does she ever see me anymore?

If she were with me now I could tell her: listen, listen to that. See, I'm not crazy. You're the crazy one for coming here, leaving everything behind – friends, family, even the dog we rescued from the home just six months ago – to live in a country where we'll never really belong. Already I am losing her. Every evening she sends secret texts from the bathroom. I hear her lock the door behind her with what she thinks is a stealthy turn of the latch. I hear her false fingernails tap-tapping the plastic buttons of her BlackBerry which she removes from her handbag when she thinks I'm not looking and slips into her bathrobe pocket. And that 'business trip' to Bahrain last week. So dismissive when I asked her about how its capital city Manama measured up to Dubai. Said she didn't see much of the place, really, spent most of her time stuck in the hotel room. I've no doubt she did.

Anger drives me on. The dune is so steep here at the peak, but the bells are louder still now and accompanied by another sound. Footsteps? The thuds are too heavy to be human. Something big. Cumbersome.

I reach the apex of the dune and peer down into the darkness, then, felled by a mixture of fear and surprise at what I see, my body instinctively drops to the ground and I burrow myself into the sand, getting as low as I can.

When I dare raise my head, I see a slightly stooped man leaning forward on a wooden staff. He wears the threadbare, sun-faded robes of the ancient Bedu people I've studied in old photographs at the museum in Bastikiya.

He is looking up at where I lay in the sand. It's much too dark for me to see his face, which is set back in the loose white *ghuttra* that flares like a cobra's hood around his head. With him are two camels, harnessed and passenger-less. For several minutes he stands looking in my direction, before tugging on a rope attached to the camels and walking on at a languid pace, fog swirling about him. There is a J-shaped khanjar dagger tucked into the belt around his skinny waist. The camels have several tiny bells attached to their harness which emit a shrill jingle as they walk. I decide I must steal one of the bells and take one back for Danielle. I'll wake her up with it. Shake it in her face until she opens her eyes. Then, when she's least on her guard, I'll tell her I know everything that's been going on, that I'm not as stupid as she thinks.

Quietly, I walk behind this mini procession for a while, keeping my distance so the man doesn't see me. I want to know where he's going, but he heads inland, deeper and deeper into the desert. There is nothing out there for miles. After a few minutes, they vanish completely, the white fog devouring them in an instant as though they were three flimsy fir trees in an avalanche.

I can still hear them, smell the animals' foul breath, but can't see them. They seem to have stopped. I sense the camels are sitting down, their bells fallen silent.

The voice, when it comes, is of someone used to being obeyed, a voice to be feared. At first I wonder whether he is speaking to me, or whether I am not alone out here. The thought of someone else lurking nearby, unseen, makes me shiver uncontrollably.

'*Yalla*, follow me.'

'Where are you going?' I reply, failing in my attempt to sound more inquisitive than fearful. 'Why should I come with you?'

I wait a few moments, contemplating my next move, wondering whether any further commands will be issued, but then I'm overcome by the need to have Danielle here with me. I must fetch her right now. Despite our relationship being no more than a warm corpse, she must be witness to my sanity, she must see what I have seen and hear what I have heard tonight. Remembering the way I came, I rise up from the sand and find myself running back to the building, discarding my sandals.

When I get to the lobby in my bare feet the security guard is talking with Danielle. She's in her bathrobe and slippers. She looks more irritated than concerned, while the security guard just stares puzzlingly at the both of us, wondering why this mad British couple is spoiling his usually quiet, uneventful night.

'What are you playing at, Gavin?' Danielle says.

'I know where the wind chimes are,' I say.

'Come back to bed,' she says, running her hand through her mess of dark hair and frowning as though I've never mentioned them before. 'We'll talk about it tomorrow.'

'They're bells,' I say. 'They *are* real, like I said they were.'

'There's no church around here.'

'Come with me and I'll show you,' I say.

'Now? No, no, I need to get back to sleep.'

'Please. It's just over there,' I say, pointing towards the dune. 'Not even five minutes away.'

She looks at me – with pity, I feel – like she did at the awful welcoming party we attended the week we arrived here and I got introduced to her new work colleagues. Smarmy Hoorays with perfect side-partings and that surfeit of confidence that comes from a private education. People with the sort of fuck-you money in their bank account that buys yachts, chauffeur-driven Maybachs and private helicopters.

And there I was. Her ostensibly work-shy hanger-on, Mr Jobless. Mr Friendless. Mr Nothing-At-All. I felt like I was going to drown in loneliness here and the first waves of social isolation were lapping at my feet. I went to the bathroom and stayed there for over an hour, locked in a cubicle, phoning friends back home, needing to hear a consoling voice, but it was a Saturday evening and no one was in. I knew by the end of that night that we'd never return to the UK together. That our relationship wouldn't survive this episode of our lives.

'Can you come with us, please?' Danielle asks the security guard.

'Not him, just us,' I say, to his obvious relief.

She tightens the belt of her dressing gown, pulls up the collar and shakes her head as she walks towards me, incredulous at her decision to play along with the irrational behaviour of her soon-to-be-sectioned, waste-of-space, husband.

'Fine, fine,' she says, shaking her head. 'But this is silly. It's so fucking *stupid*.'

I take her arm when we get outside and she angrily shrugs me off, muttering something about her meeting in the morning and her need for rest. Side by side we walk deep into the fog, and a gentle peal of bells seems to acknowledge our presence. I turn to Danielle. 'You hear it?' 'Hear *what*?' she says, but I know she is lying. Of course she can hear it. Halfway up the dune the sand claims one of her slippers so she demands we turn back, says I can show her tomorrow instead, but I tell her this must be done now. There will never be a better time. As she turns to go back, I grip her arm and this time I refuse to let her go, even though I know I am hurting her. When we crest the dune, she begs me not to go any further, says she's scared and can't see a thing, so I begin to drag her, twisting, kicking and screaming, into the midst of the fog where the stooped man and the camels await, their bells the last sound we'll ever hear before we begin our final journey.

A Home Unknown

Andrew's parents' villa is so close to the beach that he once released into the shallow edge of the Arabian Gulf a tiny cardinal tetra, scooped seconds earlier from his father's aquarium. The red-bellied fish writhed in his palm, convulsing itself into the sun-warmed water as soon as Andrew had opened his hand. He had watched it get its bearings before it darted off; a blood-tainted bullet ricocheting off invisible walls. He thinks often about the fate of that fish, recalls his father's words on discovering his piscatorial prison was minus an inmate: 'How will it survive in the ocean, boy, when it was born in a tank?'

It would have died within hours, his father told him, because of the salt in the water. Still, Andrew likes to think otherwise, likes to believe that it was somehow assimilated by a passing friendly shoal and is perfectly content somewhere out there in the vast aquatic universe.

Andrew has lived in Dubai ever since he can remember, but now he is going 'home' to a small village in west Wales. Belatedly in his opinion, his parents are trying to teach him Welsh. Though fluent, they have until now barely said a word of the language in his presence. What with the Arabic he learns at school and the Tagalog phrases picked up from Ermina, his Filipino nanny, his mother said it would have been too confusing.

He will miss Ermina more than anyone, more even than Omar and Wolfgang and Lakshita, his best friends at the International School that has filled his days for the past five years. He has begged his parents to take her home with them but she will not be needed in Wales where his grandparents will be glad to assume some of her roles, smother him with the love they have been storing up in his absence. He will pine for the vinegar tang of Ermina's chicken *adobo* which she cooks every Friday when his father returns from the rigs, and for the stories she tells him about her old life in the *barangays* of Manila. He knows that most children in Wales don't have anything so bourgeois as a nanny, that they are infinitely more 'streetwise' and that he has so far lived something of a charmed life, bubble-wrapped in this shiny, hot city where crime is as rare as the rain. He knows this because his father has drummed it into him, as if Andrew himself were to blame.

'Don't worry,' his father keeps repeating, paradoxically exacerbating what little worry existed. 'You'll be alright, *bach*, you'll toughen up soon enough.'

Andrew can count on one hand the amount of times he has been to Wales, each month-long visit a whirlwind tour of unfamiliar relatives. Barely enough time for him to get used to the roulette-wheel unpredictability of the weather, the concrete-coloured skies and the scalding-hot radiators that ran along the walls of the houses they visited. And then there was the squatness, the small scale of everything. In Dubai buildings were like long-stemmed flowers, forever climbing towards the constant sun. Under the grey canopy of Wales they showed no such mobility, condemned to terra-firma like sullen weeds.

He did like the rugby matches to which his uncle Dai took him, though. And the abundance of dense woodland, the way it changes in autumn from the green of unripe coconuts to the same rust-brown as the dates they sell at Al Rawabi's, the supermarket where he and Wolfgang buy sticky *baklawa* pastries and coconut juice. There are no forests in Dubai, no thick-branched oaks in which to build tree-houses – only hard sand and rocks, the occasional leafy oasis of a fruit farm nesting in the shadow of the Hajjar mountains.

He thinks he understands what his father means when he talks about being streetwise. One time, visiting a female friend of his parents in Swansea, he had wandered off on his own, exploring the neighbourhood. The terraced houses, with their redundant chimneys and doors that opened straight on to rickety pavements, fascinated him. He was lost in thought when two older boys had stopped to ask where he was from, something to which he had never given much thought.

'English, I reckon,' said one of them, accusingly. He wore a white tracksuit top with SCFC written across the chest.

'Are ew?' said the other, bigger boy. 'Are ew English?'

'No, I was born here.' Andrew had clenched his fists in his pockets, ready to fight if he had to, like his father taught him.

'Well ew sounds English t'me. Dunny, Cal?' said the one in the white tracksuit. 'Sounds gay as fuck.'

'Give 'im a dig,' said the one with rotten teeth, just as Andrew's Dad shouted his name from down the street, sending the two boys fleeing.

'Bloody kids around here!' said his parents' friend when he told her what had happened. 'Animals, mun. They're not all like that, Andy, love, don't ew worry.'

In his final week at the International School, Andrew passes a scrapbook around his friends, asks each of them to write a farewell message, maybe draw a picture – his mother's idea. Wolfgang and Lakshita paste beneath their message photographs of the time they went to Ski Dubai for his tenth birthday and had a snowball fight, the best time ever, even though Wolfgang poured scorn on the fake snow that was pumped out of a huge, roaring machine.

'It's not like the real thing, right, Andrew?' he had said, trying hard to impress the Indian and Arab kids. 'Not like *we* get back home.'

Lakshita, in her perfect handwriting, writes: You will be able to do this all the time in the UK, lucky thing – as if Andrew were returning to the frozen wilds of Alaska. Meanwhile, Omar draws a grainy crayon picture of the Emirates flag linked by a thick gold chain to a Saint George Cross.

'Didn't you tell him?' asks Andrew's father half-jokingly when he sees it Blu-tacked to the fridge door that evening. 'Didn't you tell him Wales has got its own bloody flag.'

'Ah, shush, Rhys,' says Andrew's mother, smiling. 'Isn't it the thought that counts?'

He rolls his eyes at his son. 'I don't know, boy, call yourself a Welshman!'

Andrew notices that his father's accent is thickening every day now, like an amnesia victim gradually regaining his memory.

While out playing on the beach, Andrew asks Wolfgang whether he thinks his parents will ever move back to Munich. His mate javelins a piece of driftwood into the waves and gazes out at the horizon, as if he might be able to spot the sugary peaks of the Bavarian Alps in the distance, sticking out like shark fins.

'I don't know,' he says with a shrug. 'I hope so. I miss my old friends. Do you?'

'How would I have any?' says Andrew. 'I've never lived in Wales.'

'But it's your country,' says Wolfgang. 'They're your people.'

Andrew slips off a sandal, burrows his foot deep into the soft sand. He thinks of two kids in a Swansea street, interrogating him.

'Can you buy *baklawa* in Wales?' asks Wolfgang.

'Not in the village, I looked already,' says Andrew.

'So... let's eat tonnes and tonnes of it before you leave,' says Wolfgang, turning his back on the sea and heading for Al Rawabi's store, beckoning Andrew with windmill arms. 'Come on, I'll treat you.'

Andrew's parents sell their furniture, give his dad's tropical fish to a friend, and ship everything else to Wales in large wooden crates, to their new home in a village Andrew has visited only once, and whose name he has only just learned to pronounce. Ever since his parents started teaching him Welsh, he has been heartened to discover that many words share the same guttural sounds as those picked up in his Arabic lessons. *Allan* and A*hlan*. *Exit* and *Hello*. Welsh and Arabic. He must be careful, he thinks, not to get them mixed up at his new school, imagines with trepidation the ammunition it might provide future enemies.

By putting an advert in a newspaper they bequeath Ermina to a pleasant Australian family, the Bensons, who live in nearby Jumeirah. She will be looking after a young boy and a girl. Guiltily, Andrew half-hopes they turn out to be what his dad would call 'whingeing gits' so that Ermina will find herself incapable of loving them as she did him.

There are no dry eyes when they drop her off at the Benson's big white house, her belongings crammed into one large suitcase and a rucksack. The Bensons promise they will look after her and, as if instructed to do so, the two children stand either side of Ermina, clinging to the sleeves of her blouse, looking like perfect cherubs as she waves goodbye to Andrew and his parents from the driveway. Andrew continues to wave from the back window of the car until it turns a corner at the end of the street and Ermina disappears from view, like a black screen at the end of a film that you wished would go on forever. He has never felt so alone.

At last, it is time to go. Andrew can't quite believe it. It only seems like yesterday that his parents told him they were moving 'back'. 'Back where?' Andrew had asked, and he had felt slightly sick when they told him.

'Cheer up, boy, it's your home too,' his father said, ruffling Andrew's sun-bleached hair with his calloused hands.

Their flight is early in the evening and from his window seat Andrew watches as a peach-slice of sun slips below the horizon. As the plane ascends steeply over the Arabian Gulf, Andrew discreetly shucks off his seatbelt and peers down at the water and the famous man-made islands that over the past decade he has watched grow and fill with houses and hotels, just as he has grown and been filled with knowledge and wisdom and the sugary treats of Al Rawabi's.

The sight of them from the air, the immensity of the structures, takes his breath away. He has heard Wolfgang's father call them an 'eyesore', an 'encroachment on nature', and an 'ecological catastrophe waiting to happen'. Words that Andrew never fully understood but knew weren't good. From his vantage point Andrew cannot disagree more. He loves the way the golden tentacles of sand poke out of the shimmering blue water, the way the villas are lined up along each frond like barnacles stuck on some gargantuan creature of the deep. They look like they've been there all along. Since dinosaurs walked the land and the oceans teemed with life.

They look, thinks Andrew, as the plane levels out and points its cone of a nose toward the setting sun, like they belong.

147

Acknowledgements

Thank you to: My brilliant and patient editor Susie Wild and the rest of the Parthian team, who punch well above their weight in the tough world of book publishing. The countless funny, smart, warm-hearted colleagues with whom I have worked at various publications in London and Dubai over the years, plus the many jesters and sages at the (marginally) less glamorous jobs who have kept my spirits buoyant when stacking supermarket shelves, sorting letters and traipsing around hospital corridors cleaning up shit and blood at ungodly hours (all grist for a writer's mill in the end). The friends who fed and sheltered me when I was an impoverished newbie freelancer in London: my old Marriott Road flatmates in Finsbury Park for late-night laughs and mice-hunting. Rob McRae – no idea where you are now but I hope you're good, buddy. Big hugs to polymath Taff and arbiter of style Chris Sullivan and his good lady Leah

Seresin for letting me flat-sit for them in lovely Maida Vale and throwing me the odd writing gig when the wolf's paws were scraping at the door. Jesse Boyce, the hugely talented graphic designer at This Is Lethal, who insisted on designing the cover for this book when I was quite prepared to beg him to do it. All the staff at Al Nisr Magazines, especially Nitin Nair, my trusty editor in Dubai, and one of the smartest people I know. Also the lovely Kate McCall and Willa King at BBC Wales for the opportunities they have given me, and Emma Bodger for expertly guiding me through my first BBC Radio play, *Jailbird Lover*. Hilary Johnson, the late Brian George, Paolo Hewitt, and Port Talbot's finest men, Neil Morris and Jared Horn. An Everest-sized mountain of gratitude goes to: Daniel 'Brains and Brawn' Morris and Delphine Joly, the former for, among many other things, saving me getting my head kicked in on more than one occasion, and the latter for being clever and French and having good taste in men. Benny Boyd for constant kindness and wisdom. Christian Reason for being solid over the years. My lil' brother Daniel, for being funny and uncompromisingly Welsh, despite more than a decade in The Smoke. Victor Romero (muchos gracias, my long-time Dubai amigo). The Rowlands family for welcoming me into their lovely home in leafy Bicknacre. Special, special thanks and much love to my long-suffering parents, Kelvin and Diane, my grandparents, Bobby and Dorothy, the late, great Rita Newton and the rest of my wonderful family, the Haweses, Newtons, Ricketts and Morgans. Finally, much thanks and love to my wife Annmarie Hawes, nee Rowlands, who tolerates me sloping off to dark corners for hours at a time to work on stuff like this. It's all been worth it, though, right?

A version of 'Zeina' appeared in the *The Rhys Davies Competition Anthology* in 2009. A version of 'Pictures in the Dust' appeared in the *Bristol Short Story Prize Anthology* 2009. A big thank you to the organisers and judges of both competitions.

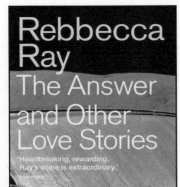

PARTHIAN

Rebbecca Ray
The Answer and Other Love Stories

'Heartbreaking, rewarding. Ray's voice is extraordinary.'

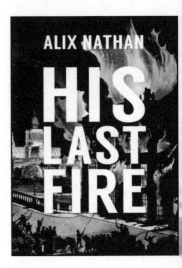

ALIX NATHAN

HIS LAST FIRE

'An outstanding young writer.'
The Times

'...raw, honest, heartbreaking and hilarious...'

Cosmic Latte
Rachel Trezise

Burrard Inlet
Tyler Keevil

Short Stories
www.parthianbooks.com